BLAGGERS

25.4.2M

Other  titles

BLAGGeRS

ECHO FREER

Hodder
Children's
Books

A division of Hodder Headline Limited

Acknowledgements: I would like to offer huge amounts of gratitude to the following people for all their help and support in the researching and writing of *Blaggers*: Robert Baron, of Krypto Securities in Leytonstone, for his patience in the face of my ignorance. Paul, of Apollo Video in Wanstead, for his knowledge of crime films. Jason, at the Lakeside Diner, for allowing me to use his identity and for proofreading the manuscript. Frank Charles, for being in the right place at the right time. And Magic Mo for her proofreading and enthusiasm. I would also like to thank my children, Imogen, Verien and Jacob, whose love and support have helped me to realise my dream.

Text copyright © 2003 Echo Freer

First published in Great Britain in 2003
by Hodder Children's Books

A Catalogue record for this book is available from
the British Library

ISBN 0 340 87568 2

Typeset in Palatino by Avon DataSet Ltd,
Bidford-on-Avon, Warwickshire

Printed and bound in Great Britain by
Bookmarque Ltd, Croydon, Surrey

The paper and board used in this paperback by Hodder Children's
Books are natural recyclable products made from wood grown in
sustainable forests. The manufacturing processes conform to the
environmental regulations of the country of origin.

Hodder Children's Books
a division of Hodder Headline Limited
338 Euston Road
London NW1 3BH

**For Maya
and Saffron**

A.A.P. xx

Glossary of Rhyming Slang

Abergavenny	penny
blister	sister
boat race	face
bubble and squeak	Greek
cash and carry	marry
china plate (also old china)	mate
chopsticks	six
Christmas Eve	believe
cream crackered	knackered
Dicky Bird	word
fridge freezer	geezer
giraffe	laugh
Gregory Peck	cheque
half inched	pinched (stolen)
Jimmy Riddle	piddle (pee)
Khyber Pass	arse
loaf of bread	head
mince pies	eyes
Mystic Megs	legs
north and south	mouth
pen and ink	stink
pony	twenty-five pounds
pork pies (also porkies)	lies
raspberry tarts	farts
Robin Hood	good
Ruby Murray (also Ruby)	curry
sausage and mash	cash
Scooby Doo	clue
sunny south	mouth
syrup of figs	wig
trouble and strife	wife

Blag: 1 n. pretentious but empty talk; nonsense (*from French: blague*).

2 vb. to bluff; to pretend to be something one is not or to know about something that one does not.

3 n. (*slang, esp. East London*) a robbery.

One

Eight years earlier

'For Gawd's sake, Alan! Why don't you just drop dead?'

Mercedes watched her father walk from the room and enter the downstairs cloakroom without responding to his wife's outburst. Ten seconds later she heard a crash as he obligingly did as her mother had asked.

The procession made its way towards the City of London Cemetery with seven-year-old Mercedes sitting in the first car, next to her mother. Her brothers were sitting opposite on two pull-down dickey-seats. Mercedes peered between their heads to the glass carriage in front of the car and beyond that to the four black horses that pulled it. She liked the way the black ostrich-feather plumes bounced as they walked. She drew her eyes back to the glass carriage and the flower arrangements that covered it. They were in every shape imaginable: boxing gloves, snooker tables, footballs, even an enormous Rolls Royce made entirely of yellow carnations. Her brothers had chosen that one. Mercedes had been allowed to choose her own arrangement and it said 'Daddy' in yellow and orange chrysanthemums. Nanny Molly had taken her to the florist to choose and Mercedes thought it looked beautiful.

When they'd been delivered that morning, however, her mother, Laverne Bent, had been less than enthusiastic. 'It's a funeral, not The Moscow flamin' State Circus!' she'd said, running round the house, frantically blowing on her nails to dry the polish. 'For Gawd's sake, Moll, couldn't you 'ave picked something a bit more subtle? West 'Am colours or something?'

'It's what the gel wanted, Laverne. She knows 'er own mind,' Molly Bent had replied tartly.

'Too bleedin' right! Takes after 'er flamin' father,' Laverne had tossed back at her mother-in-law. 'Come on, babes.' She'd given Mercedes a push in the direction of the first car in the cortège – gently, taking care not to smudge her nails. Then, just to make sure that Molly knew who was ruling the roost now, she'd added, 'You can go with Sylvie and 'Orace in the second car – all right?'

Mercedes wished Nanny Molly had been allowed

to come with her in the first car; she was getting bored. She'd never known a car to go so slowly. She didn't really understand what was happening today but she didn't like it. Daddy had gone away in the past but he'd always come home. Today though, people were acting as though that wasn't going to happen.

'Mummy?' she asked as the hearse trundled past the open space of Wanstead Flats.

'Yeah, babes?'

'What's a long stretch?'

Mercedes noticed her brothers exchanging anxious looks and her mother seemed to bristle at the question. She had the distinct impression that she'd said something wrong.

'What d'you mean, babes?' her mother asked.

'Well, last week I heard Daddy talking to somebody on the phone.'

Laverne began tweaking her daughter's fringe in an agitated way. 'Oh, yeah – what d'e say?'

'He said,' Mercedes cocked her head on one side, as she recalled the conversation. ' "You'd better keep your sunny shut, mate, or I'll tuck you up good and proper and make sure you go away for a long stretch." '

'Did he now?' Laverne gave a nervous laugh.

'And when I asked Nanny Molly if Daddy had

gone away for a long stretch, she said, "I wish he had because at least then he'd be coming home." '

'Well, don't you worry about it.' Laverne ruffled her daughter's hair.

Mercedes hated it when grown-ups did that. Especially today when Nanny Molly had taken ages tying it up into a ponytail with a black velvet ribbon. And now Mummy had messed it all up. And she hadn't even answered her question! Mercedes sat back and folded her arms, crossly.

Laverne turned her attention to her son. 'Francis, straighten your tie.'

'Yeah, *Francis*,' his brother mimicked. No one called Frankie, Francis – ever.

'Yeah, *Charles*!' Frankie retorted, knowing that his brother, Chubby, hated his real name too.

'Pack it in!' Laverne leaned across and swiped both of the seventeen-year-olds across the side of the head. 'You two is supposed to be running things now, so bleedin' well act like it.'

The twins grinned at each other and Frankie straightened his tie.

The horse-drawn hearse turned into the forecourt of the cemetery and Mercedes saw that a crowd had gathered on the pavements. Her mother gave a regal wave.

'Leave it out, Mum! You ain't the bleedin' Queen,' Frankie laughed.

A man in a long overcoat got out of a shiny black car. He was flanked by two other men and a girl who was probably a similar age to Mercedes. She had cropped brown hair and a face that looked as though she'd walked into a brick wall. Mercedes hadn't seen anyone else her age that morning, so she smiled at her from the car. The girl stared back then pulled out a large flat tongue and went cross-eyed.

' 'Ere,' Chubby pointed to the group. 'Ain't that Old Man Spinks?'

'Too right it is! Bleedin' cheek! I'll 'ave 'im for this,' Frankie said.

'I've told you two – pack it in. You ain't 'avin' no one – not today any'ow. There'll be a lot of eyes on us today.' Laverne had waited a long time for her moment in the spotlight and she didn't want anyone spoiling it, least of all her own flesh and blood.

Her mother had told her there'd be a party after the funeral, but, back home, Mercedes thought it was the most boring party ever. For a start all the flowers had gone and secondly, everyone was wearing black. She wandered outside to where her brothers were talking to Auntie Sylvie's husband. Horace Jackman was an enormous man with a shaved head. He had a gold crucifix dangling from one ear and a cigar the size of a rolling pin between his fingers. Mercedes never felt comfortable around Uncle Horace. He was the sort of person she imagined would lurk under bridges ready to waylay lost billy-goats and then eat them for breakfast. She sidled behind a bush to wait until her brothers had finished talking to him.

'So what's your take on it, Uncle 'Orace?' Frankie asked. 'I thought Dad 'ad everything sorted. It weren't like 'im to get stressed out.'

'You can drop the "uncle" now you're running things. You gotta be on top of things from the off. And you gotta be *seen* to be on top of things. It ain't gonna win you no votes of confidence calling people uncle. Your dad didn't get where 'e is today . . .' Remembering exactly *where* Alan Bent was today, their uncle stopped. 'What I mean to say is, your dad didn't get where he got . . . What I'm trying to say is . . .'

'I think we know what you're saying, Uncle 'Orace,' Chubby chipped in.

' 'Orace!' the older man barked. 'I'm tellin' ya, forget the uncle!'

Mercedes winced when he spoke but was too petrified to move.

'OK, 'Orace,' Chubby quaked.

' 'E 'ad to earn 'is respect. Now you two is lucky in some ways 'cos you can build on what Al created but you ain't doing yourselves no favours by acting all poncey and calling me uncle. Comprendez?'

'Yeah, comprendez, 'Orace,' Frankie grinned.

'Comprendez, Uncle 'Orace. I mean, Uncle . . . I mean, 'Orace,' Chubby spluttered.

'So, 'Orace,' Frankie continued, cockily. 'You reckon Old Man Spinks is behind this?'

The giant put his cigar to his mouth and pulled on it as though he was giving the suggestion a lot of thought. 'Got to be. All the aggro since Spinks tried to move in on your dad's manor.' He patted his chest. 'Not good for the old ticker.' He pulled on his cigar again. 'I knew there'd be trouble soon as we heard he was moving over the water from Deptford.'

The three nodded, then Horace pulled two more cigars from his top pocket and handed one to each of his nephews. Frankie ran his nose along the length of it, as he had seen his father do so many times, then bit off the end and spat it towards the shrubbery.

Mercedes stifled a grunt of disgust as the soggy piece of tobacco hit her in the eye. Yuck! She wiped it away and wished for the thousandth time that Daddy would come back and make everything better again. Just then she heard Chubby coughing and spluttering.

'Ugh! How can you smoke these things? They're disgustin'. I'm going to be sick! I'm going to be . . .'

And, just when Mercedes was thinking that the day couldn't get any worse, it did and he was! All over her shiny new patent leather shoes.

She ran into the kitchen to find her mother but she was deep in conversation with Auntie Sylvie, the two of them leaning against the wall.

Her mum sighed. ' 'E'd promised he was going to retire an' all, Sylv. 'E said 'e'd got one last blag planned and then 'e'd pack it in. I told 'im to drop dead but I didn't mean 'im to take me literally! I mean talk about Sod's Law – eighteen years of marriage and 'e waits till now to do what I ask. Typical!'

'And in the bog an' all!' Auntie Sylvie shook her head sadly. 'I never thought your Al would get caught wiv 'is trousers down!'

Mercedes, with an eye full of soggy cigar and shoes full of Chubby's half-digested *vol au vents*, went to find comfort from her grandmother. But Nanny Molly was sprawled on the white leather sofa with a bottle of gin in one hand, singing something that vaguely resembled 'Bohemian Rhapsody'.

Seven-year-old Mercedes went to her bedroom and decided that her family were about as dependable as a snowman in summer.

8

Two

The present day

'This doesn't make sense!' Mercedes sat on her desk and stared at the ledger in front of her. She couldn't understand it; there was a shortfall of ten pounds for that night's sweepstake. She drummed her fingers on the open book impatiently, taking care not to smudge the nail polish Fern Simmonds had just finished applying. She just hoped there wasn't a thief on the loose.

Her best friend, Jenny Logan, sat next to her. Jenny had the top three buttons of her blouse unfastened and was pushing sheets of toilet paper into her bra with meticulous attention to the even distribution between cups; she didn't want to end up lopsided. Last September Mercedes had given her odds of a hundred to one that she couldn't pull Connor the computer technician before the end of the year and she had just four weeks left. Jenny knew it smacked of desperation but an Andrex breast enhancement seemed the only solution.

Behind them En Min Lui was writing furiously to finish the Science homework she was forging for Fern. Poor little Fern had been orphaned when she was ten years old. She now lived with an ancient aunt in a flat overlooking the flyover and was hanging on to her place at the Daphne Pincher Academy for Young Ladies by the skin of her teeth. Fern was under-sized, under-achieving and now it seemed, her parents had been under-insured. Her fees had not been paid for the last two terms and Miss Pincher was only allowing her to stay by virtue of the excellent improvement in her work since Christmas – that and the dribs and drabs of money which mysteriously arrived in her name from time to time.

Suddenly a pristine twenty pound note was waved before Mercedes' eyes. The fingers holding the money looked like half-eaten sausages; fat, pink and chewed down to the nail bed. Oh great! This was all she needed. There was only one person who could be on the end of digits as disgusting as those: Harley Spinks. Harley Spinks was the original psycho; the girl who put the nut in nutter. And she was about as welcome in Mercedes' form room as fleas in a veterinary surgery.

Mercedes looked up. 'For me? How kind,' she said, sarcastically.

'I want to know what you're offering on the House Tennis Cup.' Harley's voice had all the charm of a chainsaw on metal.

'You know I don't handle sporting events, Harley.' Mercedes pretended to be checking her nails.

Harley Spinks leaned closer and dropped her voice to a threatening whisper. 'Really? Only a little bird told me you were about to change all that.'

A hush descended on the classroom. Jenny paused with half a loo roll hanging out of her bra. Fern – who had moved on to Perdita Mottson's nails – stopped, allowing the brush to teeter mid-air until a blob of glimmering gold nail varnish plopped on to the desk. The poker game in the corner was halted; the last two players clutched their cards to their chests and eyed each other suspiciously. The room was eerily quiet; the atmosphere, electric. Mercedes reckoned the odds on hearing a feather fall would've been about even.

'Well, I can only think it must have been a lyre bird,' she said, nonchalantly. 'Because I'll give you three to one on that whoever told you was telling porkies.'

A nervous titter went round the room like a Mexican wave, then died out.

'On the contrary, it was a very wise little bird who knew what was good for her – if you know what I

11

mean.' Harley Spinks was the daughter of Harry Spinks: wheeler, dealer, entrepreneur and all round dubious businessman, currently on remand in one of Her Majesty's less salubrious establishments and who, Mercedes seemed to recall, was in some way responsible for her own father's heart attack. Harley had skin like bubble wrap and breath that could have been used in chemical warfare. She wasn't just spoiled, she was putrid. If money could buy it, Harley had it – gold plated, ten times over! Including tennis lessons from a former Wimbledon player since the age of six. Mercedes prided herself that she, too, could drive a pretty mean forehand but she was nothing compared to Harley. If she *had* been taking bets on the tennis tournament, Harley would have been odds on favourite to win.

'I do realise that this is a difficult concept for you to grasp,' Mercedes said. 'But, let me put it another way – bog off!' She snapped shut the ledger.

Mercedes would give any girl (above Year 7, of course – she didn't agree with gambling for the under elevens) reasonable odds on whether or not it would rain next week, or whether Mr Duckworth would peg it before he announced his resignation. (Mr Duckworth, the Music teacher, was about a hundred and ten and Mercedes had long since ceased taking bets on whether or not he was going to retire – taking candy from a baby was no fun; she liked her punters to have a sporting chance.) She'd even been known to work out the odds on how many sneezes their form teacher, Miss Godby-Withers would clock up between assembly and break. But she would not, under any circumstances, take bets on school sporting fixtures. She'd had her fingers burned that way once before.

The previous year, she'd been foolish enough to take ten pounds from Cynthia Bigg, one of Harley's sidekicks, on the off chance that Bodicea House would win the hockey tournament. She'd thought it strange at the time as both Harley and Cynthia were in Hippolyta House and they were by far the strongest of the three house teams. So strong, in fact, that Mercedes was offering two to one on Hippolyta. They were almost a dead cert. Bodicea, on the other hand, was the weakest with odds of fifteen to one and Mercedes' own team, Minerva, were eight to one. She'd taken Cynthia's money in good faith only to discover, the day before the tournament, that half Hippolyta's front line had gone down with food poisoning whilst Minerva's centre forward had mysteriously fallen down some steps and sprained her ankle. Bodicea had romped home, winning the cup for the first time in seventeen years and Mercedes had had to fork out one hundred and fifty pounds to Cynthia.

From then on she'd made a point of not taking bets on sporting fixtures; she might be running a book on the side but she did have some scruples and there was no way she was going to encourage anyone to nobble their own players.

'Yeah, that'd be about right – too scared to take my money,' Harley sneered.

The two girls eyeballed each other. They were so close Mercedes could count the blackheads on Harley Spinks' nose. 'Well, if you really want to part with your money, Pizza-face, I'll give you twenty-five to one that you haven't used Clearasil for at least a month!' She snatched the twenty pound note from between the other girl's pudgy fingers and tucked it in the top of her black over-knee socks. 'All for a good cause.'

The sound of approaching sneezing broke the tension and Harley grabbed back her money. 'No chance!' She turned to leave the classroom but spat out one last threat before she went. 'I'll have you for this!'

Mercedes slipped down from her desk and smiled disarmingly. 'Why don't you do that, Harley? Let's say, three weeks' time, ten o'clock, House Tennis Cup? See you on court.'

'Oh, I'll see you before then, Mercedes,' Harley hissed. 'You can bet on it!'

As she strutted from the room, the class breathed a sigh of relief. Jenny folded the last square of loo paper into her bra, patted it into shape and then fastened her blouse. En Min wrote the final word of the conclusion to Fern's experiment, then passed the book to Fern and stretched out her fingers; writing in someone else's style was quite a strain on the old wrists.

'Wow, En! That's brilliant,' Fern squealed, gratefully. 'Even *I'd* think I'd written it myself.'

Mercedes returned her attention to the missing money. She'd started running the sweepstake at the beginning of the year, taking a pound per number from one to forty-nine. When the Lotto was drawn, whoever had picked the number of the bonus ball won twenty pounds and the other twenty-nine went into a secret fund. The enterprise had been so successful that Mercedes now ran three sweepstakes on both Wednesdays and Saturdays, making a profit of one hundred and seventy four pounds a week. Only this week she was ten pounds light and it was niggling her. She could hear the sneezing getting louder as their form-mistress approached. She'd hoped this would be sorted before first lesson but it looked unlikely at this rate.

'I just can't work it out,' she said to Jenny.

Jenny had stood up and was turning over the waistband of her skirt. She gave a twirl. 'Is it even?'

'Yes,' Mercedes said, absent-mindedly.

'Mercedes! You didn't even look! Come on, we've got Information Technology first lesson. This is important.'

'Jenny, he's at least eighteen. Admit it – I was being generous giving you a hundred to one. Old Godders stands more chance of getting it on with Duckie than you do with Connor.'

And then she realised! Year 9! Mercedes had ticked them off in her book but had forgotten that she hadn't actually collected the money. Phew! She closed her ledger and slipped it into her desk with a sense of relief.

Jenny was still preoccupied with the hem of her skirt, alternately hoisting and tweaking then trying to look over her shoulder to check the back of it. 'A snog you said. And I've still got a month to get it.'

Mercedes laughed. 'Yeah, but it has to be given willingly. All bets are off if I find him tied to a computer with your lippy all over him!'

The sneezing reached a crescendo and a woman of

about sixty entered the classroom. Miss Godby-Withers had a permanent nasal allergy which, even when she wasn't sneezing, made her nose twitch like some terrified woodland creature.

'Girls! I have an announcement.' Her entrance into the room had no perceivable impact on the girls.

'I'll raise you a Kit Kat,' Georgia Matthews said, pushing the chocolate bar into the centre of the table where the poker game was taking place.

'Jeez!' Jessica Johnson tossed her cards on to the table. 'I'm out!' She pushed her chair away moodily and walked over to Mercedes' desk. 'I really fancied some chocolate as well.'

'Girls!' The teacher clapped her hands to try and attract the attention of her form but to no avail.

'You can always buy it back from her at break,' Mercedes said.

'Yes, but she charges double.'

'Gir-irls!' The word was interrupted by a sneeze, which gave it slightly more volume, and Mercedes looked in the direction of the teacher. She was opening and shutting the drawers of her desk, obviously looking for something. '*Achoo*! Oh dear!' Mucus was dripping from her nose. '*Achoo*! Has anyone seen my toilet tissue?' Miss Godby-

Withers had long since ceased buying tissues in boxes and now bought toilet rolls in bulk.

Mercedes nudged Jenny who was plumping up her newly enhanced bosom. 'Jenny! Give her back a couple of sheets, for heavens' sake. She's got a bogey the size of the Jolly Green Giant hanging down.'

Jenny tutted, reluctantly pulled one sheet of tissue from each cup of her bra and gave them to Mercedes.

'There you go, Godders,' Mercedes said, handing the crumpled loo roll to the teacher.

'Thank you, dear. Now, there's a special Upper School assembly this morning. The Head wants to talk to you about your work experience placements – if only you would listen!'

Work experience! This was what Mercedes had been waiting for. She'd put two options on her form; Walthamstow Stadium and William Hill's the bookies. Dogs or horses, she didn't mind. She loved all animals, provided a rank outsider won. Although, on balance, she thought she'd probably prefer to be in on the action at the dog track rather than sitting in a bookie's office.

She put the tip of her forefinger on to her thumb to form a circle then placed them on her tongue and whistled loudly to attract the attention of her classmates. It was something her brother Frankie had taught her so that she could call the family's German shepherd dogs, Attila and Genghis. She loved those dogs and walked them every evening in Epping Forest, which was just at the bottom of their road.

'Listen up!' The room fell silent. 'Godders has something to say.'

'Thank you, Mercedes. Now, Miss Pincher wants to see you all in the hall. She has your work experience placements, so . . .' The elderly teacher pressed herself against the wall as chairs and tables were knocked over in the exodus. '. . . please go quietly and in an orderly manner.'

Daphne Pincher walked across the panelled office. She removed a large leather-bound book from the bookcase and sighed. *Spiritual Inspiration for School Assemblies* – she stared at the cover for a moment contemplating the Upper School assembly she had called, then opened the book, took out the half bottle of vodka that was fitted snugly inside the cut out pages and took a large swig. That was better!

She didn't know what was happening to the young people of today. Thirty years ago, when she'd first opened her doors she'd dreamed of her academy being on a par with Roedean or Cheltenham Ladies College. She'd even had plans to expand and introduce boarders. Now look at it! They were still housed in a ramshackle assortment of converted houses that backed on to the Central Line railway track. And, as for her clientele! She took another quick drink of the spirit before screwing the top back on and replacing the book on the shelf. The calibre of girl they attracted these days just wasn't the same. True, many were still from professional homes; doctors, solicitors, accountants, that type of family – but there was no one on her register with a title, not even a Right Honourable. And as for some of the families! Well, they hardly bore thinking about.

Catching sight of the scruffy Jiffy bag full of money on her desk, she felt her face set with irritation. Take that Bent girl! Asking to do work experience at a greyhound racing track! Daphne Pincher shuddered. She didn't like the girl – never had. She would quite happily have allocated her a placement with the Kamikaze Aerobatic Squad given half a chance. Not that Mercedes was the worst pupil at the Academy; in fact, academically she was one of those nauseating girls who was good at everything. It would have given Miss Pincher a degree of satisfaction to think that she'd achieved her success in some underhand way but she had to admit that the girl's talents seemed to be genuine. She couldn't even complain about her behaviour. True, there were rumours that Mercedes had something to do with the theft of a dozen frogs from the Science lab which were later discovered in the PE kits of Harley Spinks and Cynthia Bigg – but it was only hearsay.

In truth, the reason for her dislike of Mercedes had more to do with her family than with Mercedes herself. Daphne Pincher would never forget that morning eight years ago when that odious little man had set foot on her premises. Despite numerous references to the non-smoking policy of the school, he had flicked cigar ash on to her carpet and had continued to blow smoke into her office as he strode round reading the small print of every one of the certificates on the wall. Eventually he'd nodded and tossed a brown envelope on to her desk.

'This'll do nicely, Miss Pincher. Or may I call you Daphne?' Before Daphne Pincher had had time to refuse, he'd continued, 'My name is Alan Bent; Big Al to my friends.' The irony of the epithet had not escaped her. 'But it don't look like you'll be counting yourself in that crowd by the look on your boat race. Either that or you've trod in some doggie doos.' Miss Pincher's mouth had opened to protest but before she could speak he'd gone on, 'So, what I want, right, is for my gel to be turned out a proper lady. I want 'er to come out of this gaff with a bit of class, if you get my drift. So, 'ere's a year's money up front and I'll see you right till she's eighteen. OK?'

Daphne had drawn herself up to her full height and had been about to hand him back the envelope.

'Sweet! Now that geezer out there,' he'd pointed out of the window to a gold Rolls Royce in the drive with an ape of a man leaning up against it, 'is my mate 'Orace. Affectionately known as 'Orrible 'Orace when he was on the Island. Are you familiar with the Island, Daphne?' Assuming that he must mean the Isle of Dogs, or some other East End dive, she had shaken her head, meekly.

'I am, of course, referring to the Isle of Wight . . .'

'Oh, ye—' Miss Pincher had had an aunt who'd lived on the Isle of Wight.

'Parkhurst, to be precise. Maximum security prison.' Miss Pincher slumped down in her chair. 'So, my mate 'Orace will be the one you're dealing with on the old sausage front . . .'

'I *beg* your pardon. Sausages?'

'Sausage and mash – cash. OK? So if you've got any worries on that score, Daphne, just give 'Orace a bell. And I'll see you at parents' evening.'

But he hadn't. In fact, it had been the first and last time Daphne Pincher had set eyes on Alan Bent and (this was not something she was proud of) she had felt a flutter of relief when she'd read in the papers about his sudden demise that same week. Had it been anyone else of Alan Bent's age, she would definitely have used the term 'premature' to describe his death but for *him* she decided that 'overdue' was probably more appropriate. Her relief had been short lived, however, because at the beginning of the next term, the little girl had been delivered to her care by the gorilla in the greatcoat and had been a thorn in her side ever since.

The girls in the hall stood up as the double doors at the back of the hall opened and Daphne Pincher B.Ed. MA and OBE (in fact, Mercedes often wondered why she hadn't just written the whole alphabet after her name), strode down the aisle. She wore black court shoes that echoed with each click of her feet on the parquet floor and her black gown flapped in her wake. She had spindly little ankles that looked as though they would snap at any moment and a sharp nose that hooked over.

'Vulture at six o'clock!' Mercedes whispered to Jenny.

Daphne Pincher stopped dead in her tracks, turned on her slender heels and gave Mercedes a look which could've withered any self-respecting houseplant, then proceeded to the front of the hall. She opened her hymn book.

'Today, I will be talking to you about your work experience, which is an opportunity for all of you to go out into the world as ambassadors of The Daphne Pincher Academy for Young Ladies, whilst, at the same time, being of service to others.' She retrieved her spectacles from where they were dangling on a chain above her non-existent bosom, and placed them on her nose. 'Hymn number four hundred and eighty one.' It was her practice to read the first verse of the hymn – just so that everyone got the gist of it, and this morning she made a point of glaring in the direction of Year 10 as she did so. 'Dear Lord and Father of mankind, Forgive our *foolish* ways.' She lingered on the word foolish, hoping that it might strike a chord with certain girls. 'Reclothe us in our *rightful minds*, In *purer* lives thy service find . . .'

The subtleties of her address, however, were wasted on Mercedes: she was taking the opportunity to do a quick recce of her investments. She had money riding on the Maths teacher's, Mr Ambrose's tie; he only possessed six and his green and blue polka dot was a clear favourite. Today she was pleased to see that he was wearing the brown and yellow stripes which was too hideous for anyone to bet on, so she stood to make a tidy sum. She also noticed that Connor the computer technician appeared to be smiling in the direction of Jenny, which, financially, was a more worrying prospect. Much as she wanted her friend to see a bit of action, she was hearing alarm bells at the odds she'd offered.

Jenny, or Jennifer as her parents preferred her to be called, had been a late baby to elderly parents. So elderly, in fact, that Mrs Logan had almost made it into the *Guinness Book of Records*. Mr and Mrs Logan were now in their early sixties and their views on adolescence had never really progressed beyond their own teenage years. Mercedes felt quite sorry for Jenny. It was bad enough that at parents' evenings most of the teachers thought that Mr and Mrs Logan were actually her grandparents but, on the few occasions that Miss Pincher had allowed the girls to wear their own clothes to school, Jenny's mother had sent her off dressed like something from the front of a 1950s knitting pattern. Rumour had it that Jenny's mother and grandmother had once won the mother and daughter competition at a Butlin's Holiday Camp in 1955 and Mrs Logan now had similar aspirations for herself and Jenny.

No wonder Jenny took every opportunity her

school uniform afforded to make the most of her assets. So Mercedes didn't really mind if Jenny and Connor got it together, even if she did have to fork out a hefty sum. After all, you win some, you lose some. And this would be one bet she'd be happy to lose.

She continued to eye the assembly hall but there was nothing else noteworthy. Godders continued to sneeze for Britain and Duckie's piano playing was becoming so feeble that it made the phrase, 'tickling the ivories' seem like an overstatement. No money to be made out of either of those this morning.

Then, finally, the moment she'd been waiting for; the announcement of the placements. The list seemed to go on for ever and it crossed Mercedes' mind that the old Doberman pinscher had deliberately left her placement till last – just to make her sweat.

Jenny had got the placement she'd asked for at Kwik Fit. 'Do you have an interest in mechanics?' the careers advisor had asked at her interview.

'Absolutely!' Jenny had replied, failing to explain that the mechanics she was interested in were purely of the male variety.

Mercedes was irritated to hear that Harley Spinks' placement was at the local tennis club. No prizes for guessing who'd wangled that for her. She'd probably spend the entire fortnight practising for the tournament. Well, good riddance!

En Min had been allocated work with a graphic design company and Fern would be working in Nails 4 U in the High Street. They were Laverne Bent's rivals in the East London beauty salon stakes and Mercedes was hoping that Fern might be able to extract some insider information which would be to her mother's advantage.

But right now she didn't give a monkey's about her mother's business, she was becoming impatient about her own placement.

'Mercedes Bent.' At last! 'Boreham's Bank in St James's Square . . .'

Mercedes was in shock. What the hell did she want with doing work experience in a boring bank where she'd have to push a boring pen and wear boring clothes working with boring people? How come everyone else had got the placements they'd asked for yet she'd got tucked up with a load of old raspberry tarts? Mercedes folded her arms in anger. No way! It was at times like this, she decided, that her family might have its uses. And she knew just which member of her family was odds-on favourite to comply.

She flipped open her mobile phone. 'Chubby? It's me. Get down here, will you?'

Three

'Leave it out, Merce! Course they ain't gonna let you go down the dog track for work experience. You ain't eighteen!'

Mercedes tapped her foot impatiently. 'There must be *something* I can do that doesn't actually involve handling the bets!'

'It don't matter. Trust me.'

Trust Chubby? Mercedes would rather trust a grizzly bear to babysit her nephew and niece. It wasn't that Chubby was malicious; he was just the sort of guy who would go to give Frankie's kids a goodnight hug and break a couple of their ribs in the process.

'Well, what about Ladbrokes then?'

'Ain't no use, Merce. There ain't nothing I can do about it, sorry. Anyhows, this work experience thing's only for two weeks. You can stick it out that long. But I've got a meeting up West in an hour and I gotta go home and get changed.'

The two of them were standing in the small car park in front of the school. Mercedes was staring angrily at the asphalt, trying to think of some solution to her forthcoming fortnight of fossilisation when her attention was drawn to two large puddles forming around the bottom of her brother's trousers. Her heart sank. The odds on Chubby becoming incontinent at the age of twenty-five were too remote to consider, which left only one explanation.

'Oh, Chub, not again?'

Chubby shrugged sheepishly. 'Weren't my fault, Merce!' It seldom was; that was the trouble. 'We're on this site over Stratford, right, and I tells Gary to start breaking up the concrete floor in the basement, right. Only there's a dirty great water main running underneath!'

Following the death of Big Al, the bulk of Bent Enterprises had been divided between his twin sons; Frankie had taken over the car firm and the snooker halls, whilst Chubby ran the property development side. Unfortunately, Mercedes got the distinct impression that that side of the business wasn't so much developing properties as demolishing them.

She sighed. 'OK, Chubby, now remember when this happened at the Chigwell job?'

'Yeah, I know but . . .'

'And the Romford site?'

'Yeah, but Merce . . .'

'And we talked about the local authority plans and

talking to the building inspectors and checking where things like water mains are?'

'Yeah. And I did all that, honest.'

'So what happened?'

Chubby kicked the floor in embarrassment. 'Me and Gary stuck the plans on the wall, so that the lads could follow them and everything,' he pleaded.

'And?'

'Only Gary put 'em upside down.'

'And you didn't notice?' Mercedes often wondered how, when the twins had been conceived, their brain cells had been divided up. At times it certainly seemed that the embryonic Frankie must have taken both portions. 'Look, don't worry about it,' she placated him. 'At least it wasn't the gas main.'

Chubby chuckled. 'Yeah – do you remember that time over at Beckton?'

'I think the whole of British Gas remembers that time over at Beckton.' Mercedes patted her brother affectionately on the back. 'Look, Chubby, thanks for coming over.'

If Mercedes had been realistic, she would have realised that backing Chubby to sort out anything was a surefire way of losing not only the shirt off your back, but most of your underwear with it! She'd only rung him because she knew he thought the world of her.

Desperation had momentarily clouded her judgement. That and the fact that her only other ally in the family, Nanny Bent, now spent nine months of every year on the Costa del Sol and wasn't due back until the weekend. Still, Chubby had come when she'd asked – bless! And she was grateful for that much.

'Sorry I couldn't sort it with the old bird but, like I said, it ain't for long. Just go with the flow, eh?' He clambered up into the Range Rover that he used for touring the building sites. 'Catch ya later.' And he drove off with a wave.

The only trouble with Chubby's philosophy, Mercedes thought, was that only *dead* fish go with the flow; swimming upstream against the current was a far more exhilarating prospect. But, she consoled herself, she was going to Boreham's Bank for an introductory day tomorrow, so she'd be able to suss out her escape strategy a bit better after that.

As she made her way back into school, approaching sirens broke her train of thought. The school was directly opposite the entrance to Snaresbrook Crown Court, so it was a familiar sound to the pupils. Mercedes gave only a cursory glance along the road to watch a police convoy approaching. More interesting than the convoy, however, was the fact that Harley Spinks had appeared from nowhere and was standing by the school gate, waving as the large white prison van and its police motorcycle outriders turned into the Court.

'Your old man finally got his comeuppance then, Harl?' Mercedes called.

'Yeah, right! Your brothers wish!' Harley sneered. Then added cockily, 'I've got a pony says he'll be out by teatime.'

Mercedes hesitated. A twenty five pound bet was not to be sniffed at – but there was something about the way Harley had said it. She didn't trust her.

'You trying to tell me he's innocent?' Mercedes replied. 'I'd give you better odds on the Pope being Jewish.'

Harley Spinks tapped the side of her nose and grinned. 'Can't go down without witnesses, can 'e?'

So, like daughter, like father, eh! Just as Harley was not averse to a spot of hockey team nobbling, so her father was going for the witness-based version. Mercedes wasn't going to go within a disinfected furlong of her filthy money.

'Hey, Harley,' she said, breezily. 'Just as a matter of interest – in Geography, have you done about the Khyber Pass?'

Harley looked perplexed. 'You what?'

'Well, it's just a thought but – why don't you take

your dirty money and stick it up there!' A cheap shot, but Mercedes felt better for having vented some of her frustration about the work experience – and she knew Harley could give as good as she got.

The entrance to the school had once been the hallway of a large Victorian house and opening off it were the head teacher's office, the secretary's office and the school library. Strictly speaking, students were not allowed to use the entrance hall as a thoroughfare but it was the shortest way to the gardens. Mercedes had a quick shufti round the foyer, saw that the Doberman's office door was shut, so headed towards the back of the building. But, as she passed the library, she could've sworn she heard someone crying. Bummer! She was torn. As a general rule of thumb the Bent family motto was, 'keep your nose out of other people's business', but Mercedes didn't like to think of anyone being in distress – unless it was Harley Spinks, of course, which would be perfectly acceptable. She opened the library door and saw a group of Year 7 girls huddled by the bookshelves. One of them, a small girl who lived three doors along from Mercedes, was weeping loudly.

'Hey, Aisha, what's happened?'

'Nothing!' the others said quickly.

A bit too quickly for Mercedes' liking but if they

didn't want to talk, that was up to them. 'That's cool,' she said, and made to turn away.

'No, wait.' Aisha wiped her eyes. 'She's safe,' she said to the others. She blew her nose then explained to Mercedes that she and the others were the library team for that term. The library team consisted of a group of five girls from Year 7, whose duty it was to replace books on shelves, tidy the room and generally make sure the library was kept in a reasonable state on Mondays, Tuesdays and Wednesdays, ready for Miss Fowler, the part-time librarian to come in at the end of the week.

'There's this horrible girl called Cynthia,' Aisha sobbed. 'And she said that she'd make sure the library stayed nice and tidy as long as we paid her a fiver a week.'

'Each!' Another girl chipped in.

Mercedes' eyes narrowed. She knew exactly what was coming next.

'And she threatened to draw rude things in the human biology section,' Aisha said.

'And then she came in and knocked over the potted pelargoniums and rubbed soil into the carpet,' added Flora, whose mother ran the local florist's shop.

'And Miss Fowler said that we'd have to pay for

any damages so, in the end, we decided that it was probably easier to pay Cynthia.'

A classic protection racket! Mercedes could barely contain the vengeful thoughts that were running rampant through her mind. And she knew exactly who was going to be on the receiving end! She'd bet a pound to a penny that this little enterprise wasn't the brainchild of Cynthia. Cynthia might be Bigg by name but she certainly wasn't big in the cerebral area – unless you counted the enormous vacuum between her ears.

'Don't worry, I'll sort it,' Mercedes said. 'And if anyone – anyone at all – gives you any grief, you refer them to me. OK?'

Returning to the car park, she approached Harley Spinks.

'Ah, Harley, I've changed my mind on that little wager. What was it, twenty-five knicker? At – let's say, odds of ten to one? How's that sound?'

Harley smirked and produced a fan of five pound notes. 'Just couldn't resist, could you?'

'Well – you've got me there, Harley. I just couldn't let a sure thing pass me by.' She stuffed the notes in the front of her blouse and patted them safely. 'And the thing I'm sure of is this . . .' She leaned so close to the other girl that she could smell the salt and vinegar of the crisps she'd had at break. 'This money's going back to those kids in year 7 and, if you even attempt to extort money from anyone else in this school, you might find you need a bit of protection yourself. Am I making myself clear?'

She walked back into the library and handed over the girls' money.

Now there was just the little matter of her work experience to sort out!

Laverne Bent was poring over architects' drawings spread out on the dining table.

'In 'ere, babes. Come an' tell me what you think,' she called out when she heard her daughter slam the front door and toss her school bag on the floor.

Attila and Genghis, the two German shepherds, bounded from the kitchen to welcome Mercedes home. She stood in the doorway of the dining room patting the dogs and sighed when she saw the sample boards of fabric and colour swatches that were propped against every available surface. Having the house redecorated was one of her mother's hobbies, so Mercedes didn't give them a second look.

'There's a problem with my work experience placement. I need you to speak to the old culture vulture and get it changed for me.'

'Orright, babes,' Laverne said, dismissively. 'Look, I'm having all the salons done. We're gonna have a corporate colour scheme and I can't decide between seaspray with salsa accessories,' Laverne reached over and thrust a large sheet of cardboard covered with several photographs and colour charts into her daughter's face. 'Or –' she swapped sample boards – 'amethyst frost with opal mist accessories. What d'ya think?'

'Cool. But this is serious, Mum. The old Doberman's set me up in some poxy bank for two weeks, pushing a pen. She said they'd chosen that for me because I'm so good with figures.'

'Aw! That's brilliant.' Laverne patted her daughter's face in what she hoped would be seen as maternal pride. 'You always was good wiv numbers an' that. I remember your dad, teachin' you black jack when you was a nipper. Quick as a flash you was. Now, if I go for the seaspray, then Tara, my image consultant, thinks the name should be 'Halcyon Haze.' She placed her thumb and forefinger about ten centimetres apart and drew an arc in the air. 'What d'ya think? I'm not keen myself. Sounds a bit like a patio light to me.'

'You're thinking of halogen,' Mercedes said. 'Halcyon means peaceful and calm.' Laverne raised her eyebrows and nodded approval. 'It's also the name of a mythical Greek bird associated with the winter solstice – a bit like a kingfisher.'

A look of delight spread across Laverne's face. 'Oh, look, that's why she put a kingfisher on the logo. I get it now! And I like the sound of a solstice. Adds a bit of spirituality, don't it?'

It was obvious to Mercedes that she had about as much chance of getting her mother to speak to the headmistress as she had of training a donkey from Southend beach to win the Cheltenham Gold Cup.

'So what's your other option?' she asked with resignation.

Laverne made the same sweeping hand movement through the air and, in a voice barely louder than a sigh, said, 'Cosmic Caress.'

'Yeah, go with that.'

Mercedes had never thought the day would come when she'd say this but, for once, Chubby might be right. She might just have to go with the flow on this occasion and stick it out for two weeks. She took the dog leads and headed for the door. 'Come on boys, I need some thinking space.'

Zak Khan leaned back from the computer screen and stretched out in satisfaction. Marc Mercer, his mentor at Boreham's Bank, had asked him to prepare a financial model for a forthcoming take-over bid in the holiday industry. Timeshare Immemorial, a firm that specialised in apartments overlooking sites of historical interest, was soon to become Timeshare in Memoriam if Sunbeam. com, one of Boreham's biggest customers, had anything to do with it. Zak would've liked to have punched the air in triumph but it was an open-plan office and he already suspected that several of the more old-school fund managers had him down as a bit weird. But he'd done a top job on this one and he knew it. According to Zak's forecast, the outlook for Sunbeam.com looked very sunny indeed and, even though he knew that Marc would present the figures as his own, there was nothing that could take away that buzz of a job well done.

Zak had been at Boreham's since January and, although technically this was a gap year before going to university, he was enjoying his placement so much that he was seriously thinking about giving up the whole idea of uni. He could picture himself now, going up to receive the 'Financial Whizzkid of the Year' award. Should he wear a conventional dinner jacket, he wondered, or a white tuxedo?

'Ah, Zaki.'

Zak crashed back to reality at the sound of his full name. There was only one person who called him

Zaki – other than his parents, of course: Sukhvinder Chadha from Human Resources! And she'd placed herself at such an angle that, even had she not had the stature of your average water buffalo, it would have been impossible to ignore her. Zak lurched forward on his chair knocking the polystyrene cup that was next to his keyboard and slopping cold tea across his desk.

'Oh b—!'

'Zaki!' Sukhvinder admonished before he could finish the expletive.

'. . . bother,' he said, lamely.

'I hope you're going to mop that up.'

Zak looked at the enormous woman and smiled obligingly. 'Of course, Mrs Chadha.' What did she *think* he was going to do – add a motor and turn it into an ornamental water feature? He grabbed a handful of tissues from the box on the next desk and began patting up the liquid.

'Now, Zaki, we have a Year 10 student with us today. She'll be joining us on Monday for a two-week placement and as you are the only other person on work experience at the moment, I thought it would be nice if you would take her under your wing, show her the cafeteria, that sort of thing.'

Oh, great! Just what he needed to improve his

credibility rating; some snotty school kid to childmind. He'd been hoping to meet up with Marc at lunchtime and run through the figures with him. If he was lucky, he might even have been rewarded with lunch in the executive dining room. Instead of which . . .

'Mercedes, this is Zaki.' Sukhvinder stood to one side and Mercedes stepped forward.

Phwoar! Did Mrs Chadha say Year 10? Zak could hardly believe his eyes. This girl was seriously hot. In fact, lunch in the cafeteria had never looked more appetising.

'Hi.' He stood up and shook Mercedes' hand. 'You can call me Zak.'

'And you seriously enjoy working here?' Mercedes had chosen steak with sauté potatoes and French beans for lunch. It made a change from the M & S ready meals her mother served at home.

'Too right,' Zak replied. 'It's wicked. I'm seriously thinking of ditching the whole university thing and staying on here.'

Mercedes was poised with a forkful of the pink meat halfway to her mouth; she was trying to decide whether Zak was seriously deluded or a total geek. Looks wise, he certainly didn't fit the 'geek' criteria – and, if she wasn't mistaken, that suit was top of the range Armani. She liked a man who knew how to dress. In fact, that was one of the few things she liked about her brother Frankie. Frankie was as sharp with his clothes as he was with everything else – including his words! Although Frankie and Chubby were twins they were about as non-identical as it was possible to be. It was as though all the qualities of a single human being had been divided up; Frankie taking the full quota of brains, looks and business acumen whilst Chubby had been left with a hefty chunk of lovability but not much else.

'What about you?' Zak asked her. 'What do you want to do with your life?'

Mercedes had never really been asked that before, apart from by the careers advisor at school, and it threw her. 'Don't know really,' she replied. 'I want to travel, I suppose, but I've never really thought beyond that.'

'Let me guess, you want to go to India to find yourself.'

'Leave it out!' She raised an eyebrow. 'Do I *look* like I'm into backpacking?' She placed her knife and fork together and pushed her plate away. 'I prefer to leave the hippy trail to the hippies, thank you.'

'So what sort of places do you want to visit?'

Mercedes eyed him suspiciously. If there'd been a competition for abiding by her family motto, *keep your nose out of other people's business*, Zak wouldn't even be a contender. Didn't he know that asking so many questions was dangerous? How many times, when she'd been younger and more inquisitive, had Mercedes been brushed off? 'Them as arx no questions gets told no lies,' Nanny Bent told her. And, 'That's for me to know and you to find out, babes,' was her mother's favourite.

She remembered the time when she'd quizzed one of her mother's boyfriends (who'd introduced himself as an 'importer and exporter'), 'What exactly do you import and export, Dave?' Laverne had flashed a brash smile that was more warning than affection. 'Now, now, Little Miss Stickybeak. One day you'll poke that nose of yours so far into something it'll get stuck for good and you'll never get out!'

Mercedes had heeded the warning. Since then she seldom either asked for, or volunteered, information and yet, here she was, confronted by this seriously cute, obviously intelligent guy who was throwing more questions at her than The Riddler. And, unless her instincts had completely deserted her, his interest didn't seem to have any ulterior motive.

She shrugged to try and hide her discomfort. 'I was thinking more along the lines of Las Vegas, Monte Carlo, Tokyo, that sort of place.'

Zak nodded and smiled. Interesting! She was getting better by the minute. 'So, what made you choose here for your work experience?'

'I didn't! Anyway, what is this, twenty questions?' She checked her watch. The old bag from Human Resources had told Mercedes that, as this was just an introductory day, she could leave after lunch. 'I'm off now anyway. It's been nice talking to you.' She began to stand up.

Zak looked anxious. 'I didn't mean to upset you. I was just curious.'

'What do you mean?' she asked, the Bent definition of the word 'curious' being: nosy, snooping, interfering, meddling, spying, snitching, grassing up.

Zak was confused. 'I'm just interested. It's no big deal.'

Mercedes sat down again. Despite a lifetime of being told to trust no one, she believed him. She knew it was stupid – she'd only known him about an hour but there was a part of her that really wanted to give him the benefit of the doubt. 'Apparently, my dearly beloved headmistress is a client of Boreham's Bank and, in her infinite wisdom, she thought it would suit me down to the ground to spend two weeks of my life festering in some office.'

Zak chuckled. 'So, you don't share my love of the financial world?'

'About as much as a fish loves cycling.'

'Ah ha!' He adopted a French accent. 'So you are not familiar wiz ze Trout de France cycle race, zen?'

She smiled. He was cute *and* funny! Shame he was so much older than she was. She felt a twinge of disappointment: she'd given Jenny odds of a hundred to one on pulling Connor the computer technician, based entirely on the age-factor. Given that Zak must also be at least eighteen, was clearly above average in the facial region, had style, brains and a wicked sense of humour, she reckoned her own odds on pulling were at least ten times those she'd offered Jenny. Still, no harm in dreaming, was there? Maybe she'd even take a leaf out of his book and try this curiosity thing.

'So, what are you going to do at university?' she asked as they cleared away their dishes.

'Well, I've got a place at LSE to do Monetary Economics; learning about the financial markets, monetary policies, central bank conduct – all that sort of thing. I'm supposed to be starting in September but I'm rethinking the whole thing at the moment. You know, I'm just loving being in here at ground level, in the thick of things, learning the bits that university can't teach you.'

'Oh!' Mercedes would have liked to have asked what LSE was when it was at home, but admitting to ignorance was another taboo in the Bent household. She didn't want him to think she was stupid.

As they headed towards the lift Zak turned to Mercedes. 'So, what school is it that has one of the most prestigious banks in the world looking after its funds?'

She groaned. 'You won't have heard of it. It's this dross dump called . . .' She put on her most pretentious voice. 'The Daphne Pincher Academy for Young Ladies.'

'You're kidding, right!' Zak stopped dead in his tracks.

'No, I'm deadly serious. That's what it's called.'

'No, I mean – I know it! I went to Greenwoods.' Greenwoods was an old, established public school specialising in the academically, as well as financially, gifted end of the educational spectrum and Mercedes passed the playing fields every time she walked her dogs.

'Are you having me on?'

'No, honestly – fund managers' honour.' He placed two fingers behind his head like horns and wiggled them absurdly.

Mercedes grinned. 'So do you live round there?'

Gordon Bennett! What was happening to her? This curiosity thing must be contagious.

'Do you know St Drogo's Avenue in Wanstead?'

'Know it? My brother lives there!'

This was freaky. And Mercedes didn't like 'freaky'. Freaky made mincemeat of the odds. She did a quick mental calculation as to the chances of meeting someone who was that fit *and* lived local to her stuck in a boring bank up West and realised that she had to be talking at least five figures to one. And yet here he was, right in front of her.

'So, would you like some company on the Tube home tonight?' he asked.

And here it was again: The *F* word! Two minutes ago, she'd been offering herself a thousand to one in the Zak stakes and now he was asking to go home with her. Realistically, she should slash the odds to about fifty.

'Cool,' she said. After all, sometimes rank outsiders romped home.

'I'll meet you outside at five o'clock, then.'

Maybe this work experience thing wasn't looking so bad after all.

Four

Even better than going home with Zak, was the fact that Mercedes now had about three hours to kill in the West End with nothing but her mother's bank card for company. As she headed towards Regent Street, she flipped open her mobile to call Jenny. Could the day get any better?

For Mercedes' last birthday, Laverne had given her the ultimate motherly gift: a joint bank account in both their names. The cash withdrawal limit was five hundred pounds which, until today, had been more than enough for Mercedes. But, she realised, if she was going to give this whole bank thing a go, she was going to need to dress the part. It was a good job that her mother's signature was so easy to forge.

Laverne had never been the greatest of scholars and, before she had reached Mercedes' age, she'd been unable to see any good reason why she should waste the most valuable years of her life staring at a blackboard. It had been the mid-seventies, the era of heat waves and big hair and Laverne had spent her time working in her mother Violet's hairdressing salon, blow-drying and crimping the East Ham mod squad by day, and going up West by night. And it was when she'd been fifteen and up West that she'd met Big Al.

'You shoulda seen 'im, babes,' Laverne had once said, in an unprecedented moment of mother-daughter bonding. They had been sunbathing by the side of the family swimming pool and Laverne's maternal instinct had been lubricated with the help of half a bottle of Malibu. 'Like a mini John Travolta, 'e was. Struttin' 'is stuff on that dance floor. There weren't a gel in that club wouldn't've sold their own grandmother for a kick wiv Alan Bent.'

'Weren't you too young to be in a night club?' Mercedes had been about twelve at the time of the conversation.

'Nah!' Her mother had flapped her hand as though the suggestion were ridiculous. 'Things was different in them days. Anyhows, I looked eighteen. Even your dad didn't know how old I was till we was practically cashed.'

'Cashed?' Some of the more obscure eccentricities of her mother's language tested even Mercedes' knowledge of rhyming slang.

'Cash an' carried! Married!' Laverne had poured herself another drink. 'Bleedin' 'ell, Merce. I ain't sure this posh school's teachin' you nuffin'.'

Although Big Al had been six years her senior, Laverne had fallen in love with his white three-piece suit and they'd married, with her mother's blessing, as soon as she'd reached sixteen.

'An' it weren't 'cos I 'ad to, neither!'

The twins had been born a year later and, when Violet died, Laverne and her sister Sylvie had inherited the hairdresser's shop. With Al's financial backing Laverne had diversified, buying up other salons and adding manicures and massages to her repertoire. Nowadays, she owned eight, from Chigwell to Leytonstone and her salon in Woodford even boasted a flotation tank. Although Sylvie had stayed with the original hairdressers' business, Laverne hadn't looked back. The only slight hiccough in her meteoric rise from hairdresser to holistic therapist had been the birth of Mercedes. 'But then, that's what mothers-in-law are for, innit?' she'd said to Molly. 'Looking after the kids.'

'Sign here, please.' The woman in Harvey Nichols pushed the slip of paper across the counter towards Mercedes.

Mercedes wrote 'L. Bent' in her mother's childish handwriting and wondered how, with her lack of education, her mother had never been taken for a ride.

When Zak left the building that afternoon, there was no mistaking Mercedes leaning against the iron railings that surrounded the square opposite the bank. She had her bowling bag on her shoulder and an array of carrier bags around her feet. There wasn't a man within two hundred metres who didn't risk life and cervical vertebrae, craning his neck as he walked past.

'Hi! Shall I take some of those for you?' Zak picked up all the carriers and began to walk towards Piccadilly and the Tube station.

'Hey,' Mercedes called. 'I'm not totally helpless, you know. You can take a couple – that's fine. But I bought them and I lugged them round the West End, so I'm quite capable of carrying them as far as the Tube.'

Zak smiled to himself. Gorgeous, independent *and* spirited! There had to be a catch.

The Underground in July was sweltering and airless but, despite the fact that Mercedes spent much of it wedged under the armpit of a man whose use of deodorants left much to be desired, the journey passed in no time. There was no shortage of subjects for discussion and, instead of changing trains on to the Wanstead branch of the Central Line, Zak travelled to Snaresbrook and walked Mercedes home.

'Thanks for this,' she said as they stood outside the elaborate stained glass of her front door. The house was on Honey Drive, a private road that was separated from the main road by a wide grass verge lined with chestnut trees. It was referred to locally as 'Milk and Honey Drive' and, when there was the slightest whiff that a house might be coming on the market, it was clipboards at dawn between the local estate agents. The dwellings were large and ostentatious, having at least half an acre of garden with either a swimming pool or a tennis court – or, in the case of the Bent establishment, both.

Zak's eyes widened in amazement as he looked round the driveway of Mercedes' house. 'Jeez! What is this? A photo shoot for *What Car?* magazine?'

Mercedes' eyes scanned the forecourt at the front of the house and her heart sank. Her mother's car was there – a black Cherokee Jeep. Mercedes had never fully understood her mother's need for a four-wheel drive vehicle; it wasn't as though they lived on some remote sheep farm in the foothills of the Himalayas and the terrain up to the David Lloyd

Centre could hardly be described as treacherous. Laverne, though, claimed that she needed one, so, of course, Laverne got one. Next to the Cherokee was the silver Jaguar XKR belonging to Terry, Laverne's latest boyfriend.

Of all the men Laverne had brought home since the death of her husband, Terry Tweddle was the most odious. Terry was a market trader, although Mercedes wasn't sure what it was he traded and what market he frequented; whichever one it was, it must only operate at night as Terry seldom rose before lunchtime. Terry, or Tel to his mates – which did not include Mercedes – wore his shirt open to his navel and moved around in a smog of cigar smoke. Not only that but he carried more gold on him than Securicor. He had gold round his neck, gold on his fingers and, if he stood facing the sun, his teeth could burn the retinas off anyone who came within fifty yards. Mercedes shuddered.

Chubby's Range Rover was also there although his other car, the unfortunately coloured pea-green Boxster (his third in under a year), was not. The loss adjuster had just agreed that this, like his previous two, was a write-off and the insurance company were giving him serious grief over his plea that obstacles just seemed to be drawn to his vehicles. Trees, bollards, central reservations – you name it, Chubby's cars had had intimate relations with it.

'No wonder your family called you Mercedes – they're obviously pretty obsessed with cars.'

She smiled and took the bags from him. 'Thanks for walking home with me. I'll see you Monday.'

'Hey,' he said, as Mercedes turned her key in the lock. 'It's just a thought, but do you fancy going out tomorrow night?'

Mercedes could hardly believe what she was hearing. It sounded as though he'd just asked her out. But, thrilled as she was, she'd never actually been out with a boy before. Come to think of it, no one in her form had actually been out with a boy yet. Mainly because the old Doberman's idea of sex education began and ended with the life cycle of a toad and the only males allowed on the premises had passed their sell-by date decades ago. (How Connor the computer technician had even got past the application form stage was a mystery to everyone – although the smart money was on his CV having been upside down, so that she'd thought he was eighty-one years old.)

Mercedes' family had not exactly presented her with a wealth of opportunities to meet boys, either. Her dad had been an only child and her mother's only sister, Auntie Sylvie, hadn't had much joy on the baby front. Mainly, Mercedes suspected, because her husband, Uncle Horace, had spent so much of their marriage away on business. She'd never been able to fathom what sort of business he was in but sometimes he'd been away for years, so it was probably something to do with the oil industry, she'd decided. All in all, there hadn't been any boys in her life.

But now, here was someone actually asking her out, someone really nice and she wasn't sure what she was supposed to do. She didn't want to look like a total novice but she didn't want to appear too eager either.

'Great.' Then she had a stroke of genius. 'How about making it a foursome?'

Zak chuckled. 'Do you have anyone in mind or are you trying to tell me you've got multiple personality disorder?'

'I've got this mate, Jenny. She's really cool.' She made a mental note to talk to Jenny about being cool.

'Excellent. I'll speak to my mate Donovan and we'll pick you up about nine then.'

Nine! Her mother would go ape if she thought Mercedes wasn't even going to go out until nine o'clock. On second thoughts, her mother probably wouldn't even notice. Her brothers, on the other hand . . .

. . . needn't know. 'Nine's cool.'

'Wicked! See you tomorrow.' And he walked across the grass verge with a distinct spring in his step.

Mercedes had been trying, unsuccessfully, to get hold of Jenny all afternoon, so the minute she was through the door, she dropped her bags and took the phone up to her room.

'Merce!' Laverne's voice resounded up the stairs after her. 'These dogs ain't been walked yet.'

Mercedes came out of her room and peered over the banister.

'I'm on the phone. Can't you or Chubby do them?'

'Leave it out! I bin workin' all day. Anyhows, Tel's round and Chubby's only just got in.'

Mercedes said nothing. It would never occur to her mother that *she* had just got in too.

She returned to the phone. 'Listen, Jen – meet me over the caff on Whipps Cross Road in about twenty minutes. OK?'

The café was situated next to the boating lake and it was Mercedes' favourite haunt. She would buy a cup of tea and sit by the lake while the dogs swam after passing rowing boats or played 'chase the jogger'. By meeting Jenny there she could kill two birds with one stone, exercise her pets and bring her friend up to speed with the date situation.

By the time Mercedes reached the café, Jenny was already there, leaning across the counter grinning at Jason, the young man who ran it. Jason was the fastest fryer north of the river. He could flip a fried egg with his eyes closed and it would still land sunny-side up.

'What can I do you for?' he said, playfully, as he tossed his fish slice in the air, did a quick spin on his heel and caught it again with one hand.

'Wow, that is *so* brilliant. How did you learn to do that?' Jenny oozed, folding her arms and pushing her chest out and trying to make the most of her full 32AA minus loo roll.

'Two teas please, Jason.' Mercedes interrupted with some urgency before Jenny could embarrass herself further.

'What did you do that for?' Jenny protested as they took their teas outside. 'I was making real progress.'

'Don't even go there, Jen.'

Jenny gave a cursory tut of disappointment before sitting down and shaking her friend's arm in excitement. 'Sooo! Tell me all about them! What're they like? Where're they taking us?'

It was a pleasant evening and the two girls sat down at one of the picnic tables in front of the café while the dogs ran off into the woods.

Mercedes shrugged. 'I don't know the form on yours; all I know is he's called Donovan.'

'Donovan! Wow! How exotic,' Jenny squealed.

'Anyway, mine's called Zak and he's quite fit – and really funny, so the odds on his mate being a total dork are pretty remote.'

'Wow, Merce! Donovan and Zak! This is so exciting. I can't wait. I've told my mum that I'm staying over at yours tomorrow, so I'll come home with you straight from school. Now, have you decided what you're going to wear? I'll need to borrow something of yours, if that's OK.'

Mercedes seemed distracted. 'Sorry?'

'Clothes – you know those things we put on, mainly to try and impress people but also so that we don't get done for indecency?'

'Oh yeah – sure.' Mercedes tried to muster a smile but her voice was flat. 'Can't have you going on a hot date looking like Doris Day, can we?'

'Come on, Merce – we've got a date with two blokes called Donovan and Zak and you're sitting there like you've caught some terrible disease. What's going on?'

Mercedes sighed. 'Truth is, Jen, I think I might be out of my depth. That's half the reason I wanted you to be there with me – for a bit of moral support.' On the way home Zak had told her that he was not, as she had assumed, taking the conventional year out at eighteen while he waited to go to university. He was, in fact, only seventeen. 'It turns out that he was some kind of a child prodigy or something. He got ten GCSEs when he was in Year 9 and, wait for this, he got four flippin' A-Levels when he was only sixteen.' She looked to her friend for sympathy. 'And apparently his parents were disappointed with his GCSEs because he didn't get very good marks in Technology and Spanish.'

'Don't tell me – he only got Bs!'

'Worse! He only managed As for those but he got A* for all the rest.'

Jenny sucked her breath through her teeth.

'I know!' Mercedes said. 'The more I think about it, the more I'm wondering what I've let myself in for.'

'You'll be fine. Just don't let him talk you into meeting his parents.'

Mercedes smiled. It'd been a relief to be able to talk to Jenny about Zak but now she wanted to change the subject. 'So, tell me about Kwik Fit. Was it?'

'Huh?'

'Fit?'

'Oh – I wish! Wait till you hear this, right? There isn't a bloke there that's under about thirty. I mean they are so old they're practically cremated! You'd think they'd have a couple of apprentices or something. And you should see these gross overalls I'm supposed to wear. I mean, pul-lease!'

Mercedes smiled as Jenny regaled her with her work experiences – then her attention was caught by a conversation which was drifting out of the café. There were two men, sitting by the door. They had their heads lowered, so it was difficult to hear what they were saying, but Mercedes was sure she heard the names, Frankie and Chubby, mentioned more than once. She shuffled along the bench seat so that she could hear more clearly.

'I'm none too happy about Frankie naming Chubby as driver. Don't get me wrong, I like Chubby but everyone knows what 'e's like with flippin' motors. What's wrong with Tone? 'E done a good job while 'Orace was away.'

'There was a bit of bother with 'im and Kev, or so I bin told.'

'Kev and Tone? Nah!'

'Yeah!'

'You're having a laugh, ain't you? Canvey Kev and Tilbury Tone? They bin best mates since they was nippers. What sort of bother?'

'A bit of trouble an' strife, if you get my drift.'

There was some sniggering between the two men before the other replied, 'Well Tone's wife always was a looker.' Followed by more laughter.

Just then Jenny tugged at Mercedes' arm. 'Are you listening to me?'

'Keep talking,' Mercedes mouthed. 'I'm trying to catch what's going on in there. Although, on the other hand, we could go inside so I can hear better. I'll just call the dogs.' Mercedes whistled loudly and the two dogs bounded over so that she could put on their leads. She tied them up outside the café and then the girls went inside.

'Two more teas please, Jase,' Mercedes said.

'Here, do you know . . .' Jason nodded in the direction of the two men by the door and Mercedes got the impression he was going to introduce her as Frankie and Chubby's sister. The last thing she wanted was her cover to be blown. She was sure she'd be able to glean more information if she remained anonymous. Before he could finish, Mercedes narrowed her eyes and shook her head, silently warning him off.

'Yes, I know,' she completed his sentence. 'Too much tea's not good for you. You shouldn't go spreading that around though, Jase, you'll lose all your customers.'

She and Jenny took their mugs of tea and sat a few feet from the two men. One was probably about her brothers' age and was wearing paint-stained overalls and a baseball cap. The other was slightly older and wore the heavy blue trousers and tailored shirt of a uniform. At first glance Mercedes thought he was a police officer but closer inspection suggested that he was probably a security guard of some sort. Neither of them looked as though they moved in the same circles as her brothers and yet they both seemed to be on first name terms with several members of her family.

'There's a meet tomorrow,' she heard the younger of the two men say.

'Where's that then?'

'Dunno mate.' He tapped the side of his nose with his finger. 'Frankie says it's on a need-to-know basis and the likes of you and me don't need to know.'

The older man gave an irritated huff. 'That flamin' geezer's getting above 'imself if you ask me.'

'Well no one's arxin' you, is they?'

'Orright! Orright! Keep your bleedin' syrup on.'

There was a short silence while the two men drank their tea. 'Who's supplying the hardware? Or is that on a need-to-know basis an' all?'

'Nick the Bubble, far as I know.'

The other man nodded approval. 'Sweet.'

Mercedes was puzzled. Why should Frankie need a driver when he could, and did, drive himself? Unless they meant a driver for the car firm, although she was sure that the punters test drove their own cars. More worrying was why *anyone*, let alone his own brother, would choose Chubby as their driver? Frankie knew, better than anyone else, Chubby's record with anything on wheels. After all, it was Frankie who had to pick up the pieces – and there were usually many, many pieces after one of Chubby's mishaps.

And then there was the whole Uncle Horace episode: how could Uncle Horace have been Frankie's driver when he spent half his life away in Middle Eastern oil fields? And was 'Nick the Bubble' a name – or an instruction? Then there was the matter of the 'hardware' she'd heard mentioned. Were her brothers suddenly diversifying into computers? She hoped not – Chubby had only just mastered his mobile phone, there was no way he could handle anything more complicated than that.

Mercedes was starting to get an uneasy feeling – and it was just about to intensify.

'You 'eard 'Arry Spinks walked?'

Jenny kicked her friend at the mention of their arch-enemy's father and both girls' eyes widened.

'You winding me up?' asked the older man, incredulously.

'Straight up! Every flamin' witness failed to show.'

The older man ran his hands across the top of his head. 'I tell you, that's bleedin' criminal, that is! Should be a law against it.'

'There is, mate, there is. It's called pervertin' the course of justice and you don't get a bigger pervert in the courts of justice than 'Arry Spinks.'

Then both men rose simultaneously. 'Cheers, Jase,' they said in unison and left.

'What was all that about?' Jenny asked.

'I haven't a clue.' Mercedes was thoughtful. 'But believe me, I intend to find out.' The younger man's baseball cap was lying on the floor beside the stools where they'd been sitting and Mercedes picked it up and handed it to Jason. 'They forgot this.'

'Cheers, Merce.' Jason took the hat and called out after the men, 'Here, Gary – you've forgotten your cap!' But it was too late. 'Never mind.' He handed it back to Mercedes. 'Take it and ask your brother to give it to him at work tomorrow.'

So, Gary worked with Chubby – did that make him Gary of the upside-down building plans?

'Tell you what, Jase, you hang on to it. Chubby's not exactly made up with me coming over here.' That wasn't strictly true, because no one knew where she went when she took the dogs out, but she'd lay evens on the fact that he'd get himself into a right state if he found out. 'So, you haven't seen me, OK?'

'Seen who?' he said, looking over her shoulder and out of the window.

'Cheers!'

The two girls parted and Mercedes headed back across towards Snaresbrook with the dogs. It was all very confusing but there was one thing she was sure of: one way or another, she was going to get to the bottom of it.

Five

Mercedes didn't know what to expect from her date with Zak but, based on the way he'd been with her on the journey home from the bank, she'd offer evens that it wouldn't be the normal sort of date she'd seen other kids her age indulging in. She couldn't imagine Zak fooling around in the park with a few cans of Coke and a bag of chips. And, although a stroll up the road to the cinema at Woodford would've been OK, a frenetic fumble in the back row over a tub of popcorn didn't seem like his scene either.

'So where d'you think they're taking us?' Jenny asked, as she peered over her shoulder trying to catch a glimpse of her reflection in the full-length mirror in Mercedes' bedroom. 'You don't think this looks a bit too tarty, do you?'

Mercedes paused mid-mascara stroke. 'Jen, that's my Chloë blouse!'

'I know, it's just that it's a bit . . . well, revealing, don't you think?'

'It reveals your shoulders, if that's what you mean.'

'Yes but it's ... sort of ... well ... sexy.' When Mercedes looked up she saw that Jenny was pulling the top of the chiffon sleeves up to cover her shoulders.

Mercedes was nervous enough herself about going out on this date, the last thing she wanted was for Jenny to bottle out on her. 'Jeez, Jenny! You've spent all year shortening your skirt and padding out your bra with tissues and cotton wool and old socks and God knows what to try and get off with Connor and now, when you've actually got a date, you're acting like Mother-flaming-Theresa. What's got into you?'

Jenny's bottom lip began to quiver. 'I just don't want him to get the wrong idea, that's all.'

Mercedes instantly regretted being so harsh with her friend. 'He's not going to get the wrong idea unless you give him the wrong idea,' she said more softly.

'I know, but—'

'It's your behaviour that makes you tarty, not your clothes. He is not going to think you're tarty because you're wearing that blouse. In fact, only someone who studied at the *Woman's Realm* school of fashion design could possibly say that you were tarty for wearing a blouse like that.' She smiled reassuringly. 'You look fabulous.'

'Yeah, but my mum—'

Mercedes felt her patience running out again. 'Jen – you are not going out with your mum. Now, end of!'

The girls continued to get ready in silence. After a few minutes it was broken by Jenny. 'So, have you thought about where they might take us?'

Mercedes stood up and viewed her own reflection in the mirror. She smoothed down the Diesel denim skirt and straightened out her silver boob-tube. All it needed now was the silver Tiffany necklace Frankie and Cheryl had given her for Christmas and the outfit would be complete.

'Haven't got a Scooby,' she said in reply to her friend's question. Had she been running a book on where they might go, she thought a trip to Pizza Express would probably be the favourite. But without any previous form to go on she wasn't going to commit herself.

'Oh my God!' Jenny squealed when the doorbell rang at exactly nine o'clock.

Mercedes sighed. Had she really told Zak that her friend was 'cool'? She hoped his mate wasn't going to take issue with her on that. She could hear Attila and Genghis charging the door as though they'd been starved for a week and dinner had just been announced.

'Down!' she growled at them as she went down stairs and both dogs sank to their bellies immediately.

'Impressive!' Zak said as she opened the door. He was holding a bunch of roses, he had his shirt open at the neck and was wearing a pair of chinos. Mercedes' stomach did a backflip.

'Thanks,' she said, taking the flowers from him. 'They've got certificates in obedience training,' she explained, nodding in the direction of the dogs.

'I was talking about you,' he smiled. 'You look fabulous!' And he kissed her on the cheek.

She recognised his cologne as Issey Miyake, the same one her brother Frankie used. Mercedes felt a tingle run through her entire body as though she'd just been plugged into the National Grid.

'Thank you,' she said. Then, not knowing what was required of her next added, 'You look nice too.' She cringed. Nice? She couldn't believe she'd said that. 'I've just got to shut the dogs up and set the alarm and I'm ready.'

As luck would have it, Laverne had decided to spend the evening at Terry's and Chubby had phoned to say that he was going out with Frankie that night so wouldn't be home. It didn't take a degree in maths to put two and two together and work out that Chubby and Frankie going out together must be the 'meet' Mercedes had heard being discussed the previous day in the caff. At that moment she didn't give a monkey's what her brothers might be up to, but she scribbled a note to the effect that she was going out with Jenny and might stay over, just in case Chubby came home early. Mercedes didn't approve of lying but a certain economy of truth never hurt anyone. The fact that staying over at Jenny's would have meant going to bed at about the time they were planning to go out was beside the point. Plus, she was about as welcome at Jenny's house as a poker player at a Mother's Union whist drive! But she'd only said 'might'.

'Cool, I'll be in the car with Donovan.' Zak shook the set of keys in his hand and gave her a smile that could've lit up the whole of East London.

'You didn't tell me he drove,' Jenny said as they approached the brand new VW Beetle that was parked on the road in front of the house. 'Hey, maybe they'll take us to Southend and we can go paddling in the moonlight.'

Mercedes gave her friend an incredulous stare. 'Jen, I've just lent you my Gucci sandals. Don't even think about going anywhere near a beach in them. Just try to be cool – OK?'

Donovan got out of the passenger seat as the girls approached, introduced himself, then kissed Jenny on the cheek and moved into the back seat.

'Where are we going?' Jenny asked taking her place next to Donovan. 'Are we going in to the West End?'

'Nope!' Zak replied. 'Somewhere even better. We're going to the East End.'

'Huh?' Mercedes didn't want to sound ungrateful but, although Snaresbrook couldn't really count as the East End, her Nan never ceased to go on about when her father's family had lived in Stepney and the hardships they'd had to suffer. Returning to her family's roots wasn't Mercedes' idea of a night out on the town.

'Trust me,' he said. 'I thought we'd go for something to eat first and then maybe have a mooch over to this club where Donovan's brother DJs.'

'Club? What sort of a club?' From the way the boys were dressed, Mercedes thought she was on a pretty safe bet that he wasn't talking about a youth club.

'Ooo how exciting! We're going clubbing,' Jenny almost squealed from the back seat.

'It's not really like a night club,' Zak explained. 'Tell her, Donovan.'

Donovan sat forward and explained about the club they were going to go to in Wapping. 'It's more a sort of chillout joint, really. My brother does his set from midnight till about one thirty. There's a nice vibe – intimate.'

'How intimate?' Mercedes asked, suspiciously.

Zak gave her a sideways glance and smiled reassuringly. 'Not *that* intimate. It's somewhere where we can talk and just chill, really. Donovan's eighteen, so he's going to get us in.'

'I'll sign you in as my guests, so you lot will have to keep shtum and let me do the blagging, OK?'

'And strictly no alcohol, ladies.' Zak looked into his rear-view mirror at Jenny as he said it. 'This is not the sort of place where you want to cross the management.'

'No problem.' Mercedes knew that her mother wouldn't give her any grief about going to a club when she was under-age. After all, she wouldn't have a leg to stand on as she'd been precisely Mercedes' age when she'd met her future husband in a nightclub. But, call it intuition, she thought it was a fairly safe bet that she'd be dead meat if her brothers ever found out.

'So what's the plan tonight then, bruv?' Chubby hoisted himself up to sit on the edge of his brother's large, leather-topped desk, which was in front of the window in Frankie's office.

This was Frankie's home office and it was on the ground floor, overlooking the garden of the house on St Drogo's Avenue. Although there were some similarities between this and his office at the car yard, such as the metal grilles on the windows, a safe the size of a small house, not to mention the array of computers, photocopiers and fax machines, (in fact so much technology that neither room would have looked out of place in a corner of PC World), Frankie's home office was just that: homely.

One entire wall was lined with bookcases: shelf after shelf of leather-bound classics – Dickens, Shakespeare, Hardy, Austen. Frankie felt a sense of pride when colleagues and business clients scanned his bookshelves. It made him look better educated than his expulsion from the local high school suggested. Not that either Frankie or Cheryl had read any of them. When they'd had the house decorated before they moved in, the decorator had simply bought a job lot by the yard to give the room a touch of class. And it had worked. Frankie loved it. It was his inner sanctum; his private place where he could go to escape the harsh realities of the children's bathtime or Cheryl's nagging. He found peace in this place – usually. Tonight, though, he was agitated.

As Chubby landed on the desk, there was a sickening crunch of plastic.

'Gordon Bennett, Chubby. Mind where you're parking your bum, can't you.'

Chubby raised his bottom and removed the squashed remains of Frankie's dictaphone.

'I didn't see it, Frankie, honest.'

'Bleedin' 'ell, Chub!' Frankie took the shattered plastic from his brother and hurled it violently in the direction of the bin. It hit with such force that the bin tipped over, spilling the contents on to the floor. 'I'm laying myself on the line for you on this one Chubby, and I'm telling you, mate, the lads ain't happy.'

'I know I ain't the sharpest tool in the box, Frank, but I'll do good this time.'

Frankie took a gold cigarette case out of his pocket, flicked it open with one hand, removed a cigarette and flicked it shut again. He tapped the cigarette on the top of the cigarette case several times while he stared at it intently.

'What's the verdict on the Boxster?'

Chubby grimaced. 'Write-off and six points.'

Frankie exhaled loudly and threw his arms

heavenwards. 'I do not understand you, Chub! When I sent the lads to come to pick you up and take you back to the yard, that was your intro to keep it shut. That pukey green, mean machine of yours could've been the size of a matchbox before you could say Dinky Toy. But oh no!' He ran his hand through his hair in exasperation. 'That's what crushers is for, Chubs! We bin through this last time. The lads collect the wreck, you report it nicked, they stick it in the crusher then you sit back and wait for the man from the Pru to bring round a dirty great Gregory Peck. Now what could be simpler than that?' He took a handful of Chubby's cheek and tweaked it a little harder than playfully. 'You, Chubby. That's what is simpler than that – you!'

'Ouch! You're hurting me!' Chubby squirmed.

Frankie released his grip and then slapped his brother, not hard enough to cause pain but enough to let Chubby know that he was not a happy man. 'You go and open that flamin' north of yours and the next thing, not only is the yard crawling with cozzers but my driver has gone and got himself a chopstick's worth of points on his flamin' licence.' Frankie took a deep breath and walked round the room. 'I'll be straight, Chubby. It don't look good. It don't look Robin-bleedin'-Hood at all.'

There was a knock on the door. 'What!' he shouted.

'The kids is ready for bed. They want to say good night, babes.'

'Yeah, orright.' He tossed his still unlit cigarette on to the desk as the door opened and Cheryl, his wife, ushered in two children.

The first was two-year-old Paige clutching a piece of dirty rag to her mouth, following her was her brother, Alfie. At five years of age, Alfie had already mastered the family strut.

He stood in front of his father and met him eye to eye. 'Night, Dad.'

'Night, son.'

'Night, Uncle Chubby.'

Chubby jumped down from where he was sitting on the desk and leaned forward as though he was going to grab Alfie round the waist in a wrestling hold. The five year old moved to one side and Chubby overbalanced and landed on the floor. Paige giggled but Alfie merely looked on his uncle pityingly.

'Mummy says it's not a good idea for me to get over-excited at bedtime, Uncle Chubby.'

Chubby raised himself to his feet, rubbing his elbow. 'Right, son. I'll remember that. Good night.'

'Now then, how's my little gel?' Frankie bent down

and picked up Paige, kissed her on the cheek and put her down again. 'Bleedin' 'ell, Chell,' he said to his wife. 'That thing don't half pen and ink.' He screwed up his nose and nodded towards her security blanket. 'Don't you ever wash that thing?'

'The health visitor says the smell's important. That's what gives her her security.'

'Jeez! How can she get security from a pong like that? Security don't come in the form of smells, do it, Chubby?'

'Dunno, Frankie,' Chubby looked confused.

'Course it don't. Look at this place.' He leaned over and rattled the metal grilles on the window. 'We got locks on all the windows and doors, we got an alarm system like Fort flaming Knox. We got security lights every ten yards round the garden and you're telling me my own flesh has to get her security from a stinking piece of rag? Why, Chell?'

Cheryl shrugged. 'I think it's more of an emotional thing, babe.'

'So now you're telling me that my kid's emotionally insecure?'

Cheryl sighed. 'It ain't a big deal, Frankie. Loads of kids have them. Come on kids, let's leave Daddy alone.'

'Some trumped-up health visitor's telling me that

my kid's emotionally insecure and needs to be chewing on something that smells like you should be spreading it on the bleedin' garden and you're saying it's not a big deal? Well, it sounds like a big deal to me. Don't it sound like a big deal to you, Chubby?'

Chubby looked round the room for some form of guidance. He was pretty sure that Frankie had lost the plot, but he didn't know what to do about it.

'Here, darling. Give the smelly thing to Daddy.' Frankie took the piece of rag out of Paige's hand and tossed it in the direction of the bin. Paige let out a scream that would've shattered double-glazing.

'Here's a thought, Frankie,' Cheryl said, walking across the room to retrieve the piece of fabric. 'Next time you decide to make her go cold turkey on the whole security blanket thing, do it when you're the one's looking after her and I'm the one going out on the town for the night, eh?' She picked up Paige and gave her the rag. The two-year-old stopped crying immediately. 'You'll probably still be sucking it when you're sixteen, if we wait for that, won't you darling?' And she left the room with both children.

'Gordon bleedin' Bennett, Chubby. You are definitely better off being single, mate, I'm telling you. Trouble and strife ain't the half of it! She knows we got a meet tonight. Anyone would think we was going out socialising the way she goes on.' He picked up the unlit cigarette from the desk, flicked open his gold lighter and blew out a plume of smoke. 'Right then. Fancy a Ruby before we meet the lads?'

Six

'Can I borrow your lippy?' Jenny asked as they stood in the ladies' toilet of the Pizza Express where the boys had taken them. She turned to face the mirror and gave a shiver of excitement. 'He's a bit gorge, isn't he?'

Mercedes smiled and took her lipstick out of her bag. 'They're both really cool.' She was still mentally congratulating herself on having successfully picked the right restaurant. Maybe she wasn't losing her touch after all.

'So, that's two hundred quid you owe me.' Jenny was applying the lipstick and eyeing Mercedes in the mirror.

Mercedes raised an eyebrow. 'How do you work that one out?'

'Well, I put two quid on pulling an eighteen-year-old and you gave me a hundred to one. You're not the only one who can do maths you know, Merce.'

'OK,' Mercedes said, taking back her lipstick. 'Point one is that the bet was on pulling Connor and not just any old eighteen-year-old who happened to wander into your life. Point two is that you haven't *pulled* Donovan, you're on a blind date with him. You can't move the finishing line to suit yourself, you know.'

'Woooo! That's a bit harsh isn't it?' Jenny looked hurt.

'No Jen – it's life. Now come on. They'll think we've fallen down the pan we've been in here so long.'

She dropped the lipstick into her bag and gave her reflection the once-over in the mirror. Mercedes knew that, like her mother before her, she could easily pass for eighteen. She wasn't so sure about Jenny though. Even with the Chloë top and Gucci sandals, Jenny still only looked her age.

'Jen,' she said as they left the toilet, 'when we get to the club, if anyone asks you your date of birth, remember to knock three years off, OK?'

Jenny stared questioningly at her and then said, 'Wouldn't that make me only twelve?'

Mercedes sighed. No wonder Mr Ambrose had suggested that Jenny took the lower paper in Maths. 'Don't think about it, just do it, OK?'

The club was around the corner from the restaurant, so they left the car and walked. Jenny and Donovan were walking ahead and Mercedes could hear Jenny laughing and chatting as though the battery on her voice box was going to run out at any moment. Mercedes and Zak were walking some way behind. The night was sultry and Zak was telling her about his family and how his father and uncle were both merchant bankers. If, two days ago, someone had bet her that she would be walking through the cobbled streets of Docklands accompanied by the most gorgeous boy she'd ever set eyes on, she would have given them better odds on man flying to Jupiter under his own wing-power. She could hardly believe that it was real.

She checked her watch; it was eleven thirty.

'Are you OK?' Zak asked, placing an arm round her shoulders.

'I'm fine.' She took out her mobile phone and turned it off. Not that there was the remotest chance of her mother phoning to make sure she was all right, but the last thing she wanted was Chubby calling to check up on her.

'OK, just act naturally,' Donovan said, as they turned down a narrow alley between two blocks of warehouses towards the river. There was a neon sign ahead and Mercedes could just make out the name, the Terra Firma.

'Weird name for a club, isn't it?' Jenny commented

as they drew closer. 'It's like calling a club The Terror Company. Who in their right mind would want to call a club that?'

Mercedes looked at her friend trying to work out whether or not she was being serious. 'Are you having us on? *Terra firma*'s Latin. It means solid ground.'

'Oh.' Jenny giggled, unembarrassed by her *faux pas*.

'This was probably a pub in the olden days when Wapping was a port. The sailors must have moored here and practically fallen off the boats and into the pub and solid ground.'

'Nah!' Donovan interjected. 'I think Jenny's right. My brother says this place is run by a right load of dodgy geezers.'

'That's why I said we didn't want to upset the management,' Zak reiterated. 'Call me a wuss but scuba diving in concrete flippers isn't my favourite water sport.'

'Oh great!' Mercedes folded her arms angrily. 'Well call *me* a wuss but dicing with dodgy geezers isn't exactly my idea of a fun night out either. What the hell were you thinking of, bringing us here?'

'I think it's exciting,' Jenny said.

'Exciting? Jeez, Jen!' Mercedes slapped her

forehead. 'Who's the dodgiest fridge we've heard of?'

Jenny looked perplexed. 'Well, my mum had a Zanussi that went on the blink.'

'Huh?' Then realising that Jenny was not as familiar with rhyming slang as she was, Mercedes explained, 'Fridge freezer – geezer!'

Jenny rolled her eyes. 'Oh! Seriously, Mercedes – I think you've been mixing with your family too much.'

'Anyway, to get back to my point,' Mercedes said. 'Dodgy geezer – Harley Gravel-face Spinks' dad?'

'Oh my god! I hadn't thought of it like that.'

'Well, start thinking of it like that! Now start thinking what some dodgy bloke like Harry Spinks might do if he found two under-age girls in one of his clubs.'

Jenny gave a whimper.

'Exactly!'

'Hey, ladies,' Donovan interrupted. 'Chill! I've been here loads of times and I've never had any grief.'

'Now, why do you think that is, Donovan?' Mercedes asked. 'Perhaps because you're *not* under-age?'

'It'll be cool,' Zak put his arm round her shoulder again. 'I wouldn't have suggested this place if I'd thought it was a problem.'

'Just keep a low profile and don't make it obvious that you're not eighteen – that's all,' Donovan added.

Mercedes shot Jenny a warning glance and the group walked on in silence. Zak's arm around her went someway towards placating her but Mercedes was still angry. She'd stay for about half an hour, she decided, and then ask to be taken home. Going to a club was one thing but, if her brothers ever found out that she'd been frequenting a suspect club run by some Harry Spinks-type villain, then it wouldn't just be the management who'd be on her case. She might as well pack her bags and enter a convent now. And Zak . . . well, she daren't even *think* what they'd do to Zak.

There was a small queue of people waiting outside but Donovan walked straight to the front. He stepped forward and grabbed one of the bouncers hand to forearm and slapped him on the back. 'Hey! How you doing, man?' he asked jovially.

'Oooo! This is quite exciting though, isn't it?' Jenny whispered in Mercedes ear as they waited for Donovan to get them in.

'Jen – cool it,' Mercedes almost snapped. 'Just act like we do this every Friday night.'

'Hey! Dono!' The man was the size of a medium-sized furniture van and was dressed from head to toe in black.

'Oh my god! I wouldn't like to meet him down a dark alley at midnight,' Jenny said.

Mercedes gave her friend an incredulous look. 'For starters we *are* down a dark alley at midnight – durrr! And coming in a close second – I think there was a guy on the top of Canary Wharf who didn't quite catch that. Maybe you could use a megaphone next time?' She was beginning to think that the concept of 'keeping a low profile' was beyond Jenny.

The bouncer returned Donovan's friendly slap on the back. 'You on the guest list, man?'

'Too right, mate!'

'OK – later!' The bouncer laughed and waved the group through. 'Donovan plus three,' he called to a woman who was sitting in the ticket office chewing gum.

'Cheers.' The woman didn't even look up as she ticked off Donovan's name from a list in front of her and ushered them straight through.

'Piece of cake!' Donovan grinned as he led them through a bead curtain into the dim interior of the club. 'Now, am I the man, or am I the man?'

Mercedes felt relieved to have successfully negotiated the doorman and was beginning to pick up on Jenny's excitement. She looked round in awe. The room was small and, as Zak had said, intimate. The decor was high kitsch pseudo-Egyptian. Secluded alcoves surrounded a central dance floor, each individually decorated with mummies and hieroglyphs. Some were accessible only by small flights of stairs and overlooked the main area. A jewelled sphinx stood at each corner of the bar and, adjacent to it, the DJ box was shaped like a Tiffany-style coloured glass pyramid.

'Penny for them?' Zak smiled.

'Are you kidding? What sort of a girl do you think I am, selling my thoughts for a mere Abergavenny?' she laughed.

'You lot sit down,' Donovan instructed. 'I'll get the drinks. Coke OK?'

'I'd like a pineapple juice over mineral water, please,' Mercedes said. 'In a tall glass with plenty of ice and a slice of lime.'

Zak smiled to himself. She was certainly a girl who knew what she wanted. He liked that. None of this saying things just to please other people. At least you knew where you were with someone like that.

'Make that two,' Jenny added.

'I'm cool with a Coke,' Zak called after him. 'Full fat though – I don't want any of that diet stuff.'

They chose one of the bays that was up a spiral staircase and occupied a corner. From their vantage point they could see most of the club but would be concealed from the other punters. A few people were dancing but not many. The music was more ambient trance than dance and most people were either sitting or standing in groups, talking.

'Now do you see why I wanted to bring you here?' Zak shuffled round the bench seating until he was closer to Mercedes. 'Isn't it amazing?'

'Caesar's Palace,' she said, absently. 'It reminds me of pictures of Las Vegas – only better.' Mercedes imagination was running wild. 'I could start with something about this size and do it out like this. I'd have card games in the niches and the main floor space for roulette. It would be perfect to start off with.'

He picked up her hand in his and squeezed it gently. 'I can see we'll have to watch you once you start work at the bank.'

'Why's that?' she asked.

'Didn't you notice the building work next door?'

It was true that Mercedes had seen the scaffolding on the building next to Boreham's Bank, but it had seemed such an unimportant fact that she hadn't even questioned it.

'It's going to be a swanky gaming club, apparently,' Zak enlightened her. 'Who knows, in a couple of years' time, you might be applying for a job there.'

Mercedes smiled. 'You don't know me very well, do you. I won't be applying to work there – I'll be looking to own it!'

Donovan came back with both the drinks and his brother, Dylan. They both seemed perturbed. 'Here you go,' Donovan said, putting down the drinks on the table. Dylan was in his early twenties and was the spitting image of his brother except that Donovan's hair hung in dreadlocks and Dylan's head was shaved. He rested his hands on the edge of the table and leaned forwards towards the group.

'OK, folks, this is the situation. The management's entertaining in-house tonight so it's best for everyone if you keep your heads down. They don't like aggro and the slightest whiff of anything that might alert the Old Bill and my job's on the line. I know Dono's eighteen but the four of you were on my guest list, so any grief and it's me that gets it.'

'We're fine just to stay up here,' Zak reassured him.

'Cool. I'd better get back – my set starts in five minutes.' Then Dylan stopped. 'Bummer! That's them now.' He pointed to a group of four men who had just entered the club through a side door next to the DJ box. 'The two blokes nearest us are the owners and the big guy at the far side is the manager. Believe me, they are not nice people so just keep out of sight.'

Mercedes leaned forward to catch a glimpse of these *not nice* people who seemed to rule their staff through terror. A sickening stab of recognition shot through her. There beneath her, in the middle of the dance floor, she saw not Harry Spinks and his heavies (whom she had mentally put at four to one favourite), but none other than her own brothers, Frankie and Chubby.

'Oh! My! G—' Jenny looked across the table; her eyes wide with shock.

A sharp kick on the shin from Mercedes stopped her mid sentence.

'G— ow . . . oh . . .' Jenny's voice trailed away.

Although Jenny had never met Frankie, she knew Chubby and had obviously recognised him, so Mercedes narrowed her eyes, silently warning her to keep quiet. How anyone with even half a gram of social awareness could even think of revealing that one of those men was Mercedes' blood relation, was beyond belief. It was something Mercedes was having difficulty getting to grips with herself. She certainly didn't want Jenny blabbing it to Zak and Donovan on a first date. What the hell had she been thinking? But, more to the point, what did it mean? There must have been some sort of mistake. How could anyone have thought of Chubby in those terms anyway? Chubby wouldn't swat a fly. Frankie, on the other hand . . . Well, she could believe anything of Frankie – almost. But not this. She knew he could be a bit creative about his business dealings but the insinuation had definitely been that the owners were on the fringes of crime.

'Jeez!' Zak leaned forward peering at the group below them. 'That guy lives just down the road from me.'

Great! So her best friend recognised one brother and her boyfriend recognised the other. At least Zak didn't know that Frankie was related to her. She leaned back trying to distance herself from what was unfolding.

But things were about to get worse.

The man whom Dylan had described as the manager turned slowly in a circle as though doing a recce of the club. His gold crucifix earring caught the light and, with a dull thud of recognition, Mercedes saw her Uncle Horace. Oh deep joy! Who was going to come crawling out of the woodwork next, she wondered? Her mother, perhaps? Or even Nanny Molly? Talk about Sod's Law! Her first time deviating from the straight and narrow and her family had turned out in force to try and catch her out.

She watched as her brothers followed Horace's lead, looking round the club; scanning the punters for . . . For what? Under-age drinkers? No way! Even Mercedes wasn't that naïve. No, the previous day's overheard conversation combined with this and she had the feeling that something big was going down. But what? She didn't like it. She didn't like it one bit.

'Are you OK?' Zak asked.

'I'm fine,' she replied, unconvincingly. 'Bit of a headache, that's all. I'll just sit here and finish my drink.'

Or maybe, she thought, there was a slim chance that she'd fallen asleep and woken up in the middle of a bad dream. Her eyes scanned the club trying to find evidence that the whole thing was a misunderstanding; that her brothers weren't the people Dylan had been talking about. She knew her brothers were a bit overprotective with her and she knew they weren't averse to accepting the odd backhander every now and again but that didn't make them crooks, did it? Five minutes ago she'd been worried about what her brothers would say if they knew she'd been to a club that was run by criminals; now she was being told that her brothers *were* those criminals. It was too much to take in. She needed to get out and go home but her only exit was across the floor where she'd be seen by the very people she wanted to avoid.

'Do you want to go home?' Zak looked concerned.

'No!' she said, meaning, Yes but only if you can wave a magic wand and beam me out of here without us having to cross the dance floor. 'I'll just sit back and take it easy.'

From the back of the alcove she could watch her brothers and wait for an opportunity to make her escape and she was fairly certain that they couldn't see her. She saw Frankie nod in the direction of an alcove that was concealed from the main area by a fretwork screen. It was diagonally opposite their hiding place. Her brothers walked towards it and the fourth man in the group stepped forward and pulled back the screen. He was smaller than the others, of Mediterranean complexion and was completely unknown to Mercedes. She felt a momentary flush of relief that at least there was one member of the group who wasn't related to her by either birth or marriage.

Dylan had begun his set and the music had increased in tempo. More people were taking to the dance floor.

'Shall we have a dance?' Jenny asked Donovan.

'Er, hello!' Mercedes pointed out. 'Has the whole low-profile business gone by the board?'

'Come on, no one will see us. There's so many people down there.'

93

For once Mercedes thought that Jenny might have a point. The dance floor was quite crowded and, with her brothers otherwise engaged with their meeting this could be ideal time to make their exit.

'Actually,' she said to Zak, 'I think I would like to go home now.'

Jenny opened her mouth to protest but another look from Mercedes stopped her.

Mercedes sent the boys down the spiral staircase first and she and Jenny followed. Once they were on the dance floor she felt safer. They merged with the other clubbers and, in the subdued lighting, she was sure they were home and dry. Zak took her hand. Halfway across the room he stopped.

'Sure you don't fancy dancing?'

It was very tempting but, as she paused to consider his suggestion, she felt a strange hand between her shoulders. Despite the heat, an icicle of fear slithered down her spine, as she was pushed forwards into Zak's chest.

'OK,' he grinned. 'If you're asking, I'm dancing.' And he placed his arms round her waist.

'What the hell happened?' she asked angrily, peering over his shoulder to try and see who it was who'd pushed her.

'There was a woman on a mission and it seemed that you were in her path.'

Mercedes peered through the crowd to a woman crossing the dance floor. She was slim and black with long weaves to her waist. She walked slowly, wrapping one leg in front of the other with her head high and the expression of a wild cat stalking its prey. The dancers parted like the waters of the Red Sea, as she made her way towards the booth in the corner.

Zak leaned forwards and shouted into Mercedes' ear, 'Hey! You've been slapped on the back by Honey Coombes, the supermodel.'

'Great, I'll never wash my shoulder blades again,' she replied, distractedly.

She watched as the model tapped on the fretwork and waited for the wooden screen to be pulled back. Honey Coombes was glaring round the room and tapping her stilettoed foot impatiently. Frankie emerged from the alcove, placed his arm around her waist and kissed her full on the lips. Any anxiety Mercedes had felt about being caught in a club was suddenly replaced with outrage. The dirty rotten cheat! And how could Chubby sit there and go along with his brother's two-timing, scumbag antics?

Once more, Zak leaned forward so that Mercedes could hear him above the music. 'Wow! That's the guy who lives near me and, unless his wife's been overdoing it on the sunbed, it looks like he's playing away from home. I think you're right – it's probably best that we get out of here. If he's as dodgy as Dylan's making out, I've got more information than is healthy for someone who'd like to make it to his eighteenth birthday.'

Just at that moment, Mercedes saw Honey push a piece of paper into her brother's top pocket and then point in the direction of the door. She appeared to say something to Frankie. Mercedes watched her brother strain his neck, looking over the heads of the dancers. Mercedes wasn't scared of being found out any more – she had enough inside information now to keep Frankie quiet – but she was intrigued to know exactly what was going on. Frankie put his fingers to his lips, the way he had taught Mercedes to do when she wanted to call the dogs, and let out a whistle that could penetrate a thousand decibels of music. Then he beckoned in the direction of the door.

Keen to remain unseen, Mercedes grabbed Zak, pulled him towards her and kissed him. It wasn't quite how she'd planned her first kiss. After all, it wasn't exactly romantic; her attention was focused more on what was going on over his shoulder than what was going on in their mutual lip area. But she'd always prided herself on being able to multi-task.

The bouncer who had let them in crossed the floor and faced Frankie. There was a brief altercation during which Frankie appeared to grab the front of the bouncer's trousers. He sank to his knees, said something to Honey who gave a haughty sniff before entering the private booth with Frankie and leaving the bouncer on the floor.

Mercedes pulled away from Zak. 'Thank you,' she said.

Zak looked dazed. 'Wow! My pleasure!'

'Cool!' Mercedes smiled and headed towards the exit.

Well, one thing was certain anyway; Frankie could scream and holler all he liked about her being in a club under-age but he was on a hiding to nothing now. He wouldn't dare say a word. OK, so some people might call it blackmail, but Mercedes preferred to think of it as her safety net. And she was going to use whatever means she could to discover exactly what was going on in her family.

Seven

Watching grass grow would've been infinitely more exciting than Mercedes' weekend. Apart from Jenny wanting to know why Donovan hadn't phoned her, (eight times), and En Min wanting to find out how the date had gone, Mercedes' mobile might as well have dropped into a sound-proofed well for all the messages she got from Zak.

The house phone, on the other hand, had hardly stopped ringing. Nanny Molly was due into Stansted on the Sunday evening, combining her summer respite from the Costa-del-Lager-and-Chips holidaymakers with her seventieth birthday celebrations the following weekend. The marquee had been ordered, the caterers briefed and guests invited – yet, by mid-afternoon on the Sunday, Mercedes was in danger of developing a permanent crick in her neck from having taken so many telephone messages. The sound of it ringing again was too much. She folded her arms, lay back on her bed and let it ring.

'Get it for us, will ya, babes?' Laverne called from where she and her sister were sitting on loungers by the poolside, apparently incapable of reaching out to the cordless phone that was less than an arm's length from either of them.

Mercedes remained resolute. It wouldn't be anything important anyway. By which she meant that it wouldn't be the one person she wanted it to be. The odds on Zak ringing on the landline were at least a thousand to one. There was no way she'd ever give him her home number – just on the off chance that her mother might pick up. Although, in the light of this weekend's phone activity, there'd be fat chance of that happening.

She put her hands behind her head and stared idly at the ceiling as she worked out the odds on a variety of telephone contenders. Over the course of the Saturday, she had taken three calls from And So to Bedouin, the tent people, triple-checking Laverne's constantly changing instructions on the size of the marquee. Florrie's Flowers had rung, confused about the number of table centre-pieces and Helium Heaven had called to say that they needed to take expert advice as to whether or not the marquee would stay moored to the ground with so many balloons inside it. Being Sunday, Mercedes was fairly certain that she could write off anyone concerned with the party as a rank outsider.

'Merce! Get the bleedin' phone for gawd's sake, will ya?'

Mercedes was well and truly fed up with being her mother's secretary. 'Can't you get it?' she called down from her bedroom window.

'You 'aving a giraffe, or what?' came her mother's truculent reply. 'Can't you see Sylv's doing my nails!'

Mercedes flopped back on to her pillow just as the phone stopped ringing. So what? If it'd been important they'd leave a message on the answerphone. Her nan had already phoned both as she'd left her apartment in Marbella and again from the airport in Malaga and, according to Ceefax, air-traffic controllers across Europe were on their best behaviour, so it wasn't likely to be anything urgent. Mercedes carried on where she'd left off working out the tote: Frankie hardly ever rang so she'd give him fifty to one. Cheryl on the other hand, having been brought up in care herself, seemed to be under the misapprehension that her mother-in-law was the childcare guru of East London, and was a distinct possibility worth at least five to one. But, Mercedes gave a shudder, the fingers-down-the-throat favourite at two to one on, had to be Terry Tweddle. And no way was she up for a conversation with Gold Denture!

'Who was it?' her mother's voice sounded from the garden.

'Dunno!'

'What d'ya mean?'

Mercedes wondered why they'd bothered booking an amplifier for next Saturday's party – all they needed to do was plug the PA system into her mother and the whole of Snaresbrook would get an earful.

'It stopped before I could get it.'

She heard her mother mutter something to Auntie Sylvie. Then, 'Come down 'ere, will you.'

Mercedes, still hopeful that Zak might ring, picked up her mobile and went into the garden. Laverne was holding her fingers out as though she'd had steel rods inserted.

'Look, babes! What d'ya think?' Each nail, long enough to be called a talon in any other species, had a crescent of black nearest the nail-bed with a silhouette of a palm tree against a gold and pink sunset. 'Reminds me of Lanzarote last year, don't you think, babes? Sylv's done them with transfers for now – just so as I can get a feel for them and then I'll get Angie at the Chingford salon to airbrush them next week. Fabulous, ain't they?'

Mercedes found it difficult to match her mother's

enthusiasm. 'Lovely,' she said with more obligation than admiration.

'Now, what d'you think about a diamanté stud in the middle of each sun?'

Mercedes sighed. It was time for truth to prevail over diplomacy. 'Too much.'

'Yeah, I think she's right, 'Verne,' Sylvie agreed. 'I would just have one on each thumb if I was you.'

'I'm going to take the dogs out before Nan gets here.'

'What about the phone?' Laverne asked.

'What about it?'

'Ain't you gonna do 1471 and see who it was?'

Mercedes stood for a moment without answering. She wanted some space. So much had happened in the past seventy-two hours. Her whole perspective on life had done a hand-brake turn and she needed to make sense of it all. She'd met, gone out with and kissed the most gorgeous boy she'd ever set eyes on but now he hadn't either phoned or replied to any of her text messages. She'd also discovered that her brothers were involved in some sort of underhand activities and, the more she thought about it, the more she realised that her mother probably knew all about it too. Uncle Horace was obviously up to his neck in it, so unless he and Auntie Sylvie had a totally non-communicative relationship, she suspected that her aunt was also a party to the dubious dealings. She knew that she'd been brought up to trust no one, but she'd never dreamt that that included her own family.

Ignoring her mother's question she turned to her aunt. 'Auntie Sylvie, what does Uncle Horace do?'

An almost imperceptible glance passed between the two sisters before Sylvie found something that required her full attention on Laverne's thumb nail. 'A bit of this; a bit of that. You know,' she said, without looking at her niece.

'No, I don't know,' Mercedes persisted. 'A bit of what?'

'He's a consultant,' Laverne chipped in. 'Now, go do 1471, there's a good gel.'

'What sort of consultant?'

'Who d'you think you are, Chris bleedin' Tarrant?' her mother snapped.

'It's just that he seems to work away from home quite a lot.'

'Yeah, and?'

Satisfied that there was something definitely fishy about her uncle's employment that her family didn't want her to know about, Mercedes realised that it would be impossible to investigate further without giving away the fact that she'd been in the nightclub.

'I just wondered if he'd be home for Nan's party, that's all.'

Another glance passed between the sisters, this time one of relief. 'Course'e will, darlin',' her aunt smiled. 'Orace wouldn't miss it for the world.'

'Now, babes, go get the phone and find out who was calling will you?'

'No,' she said. 'I told you, I'm going to take the dogs out.'

Unused to such non-compliance both Laverne and Sylvie stared open-mouthed.

'Why, you cheeky little mare!' Laverne said, after some time.

Ignoring her mother, Mercedes whistled through her fingers and the dogs bounded down from the shrubbery behind the tennis court. She turned and walked towards the house.

'Merce! You come back 'ere!' Her mother was flapping her hands and shouting.

'Watch it 'Verne – the top coat ain't dry yet,' Sylvie warned.

'Merce! Get back 'ere! What's got into you, you mouthy little cow?'

Mercedes took the dog leads from the hook by the door and switched off her mobile. She did not want to be contacted by anyone. And if Zak rang – well, too bad! He should've rung sooner. From now on, no one was going to mess with Mercedes Bent. And she meant no one!

Zak paced up and down the pavement in St James's Square. It was almost five to nine and he'd been there since just turned eight o'clock. Surely he couldn't have missed her. Sukhvinder Chadha rounded the corner, so he dodged behind one of the skips from the building site next door to avoid being seen.

'I'm neither blind nor stupid, Zaki. You have five minutes to be at your workstation. Do not be late.' She didn't even pause as she strode up the steps into the bank.

Bummer! He would just have to wait until lunchtime and hope that he could catch Mercedes then. The sense of frustration that had been brewing all weekend overflowed and he kicked the side of the skip, then hopped backwards as an agonising pain seared from his big toe, along his foot and up his shin bone.

'Oi!' a voice shouted from the scaffolding above. 'Go kick your own bleedin' skip.'

'Sorr—' As Zak shouted his apology, the man's hard hat crashed on to the pavement, narrowly missing Zak's head. He let out a low whistle of relief at this near miss. Bending down to pick up the hat he heard a chorus of catcalls and wolf whistles from the workmen above. He looked up and saw the focus of the men's attention; a pair of legs was coming towards him, long and tanned with a gold, two-tier ankle bracelet he would recognise anywhere. His heart missed a beat. He straightened up and beamed as Mercedes approached. She was wearing the Burberry suit she'd told him she'd bought and she looked gorgeous.

'Hi. I'm so glad I've caught y—' His voice trailed away as Mercedes walked past with no hint of recognition. 'Mercedes, wait! Let me explain, please.' He hurriedly hobbled after her, inadvertently clutching the workman's helmet in his hand.

She stopped on the stone steps up to the bank and faced him full on. 'Explain or excuse?'

Zak looked her in the eye. God, she was fantastic! The way her eyes sparkled and the way her hair shimmered in the sunlight. He felt his stomach tense and he swallowed, trying to control his voice. 'I had my phone nicked and I'd put your number straight into it.'

'Yeah, right!'

She turned away but he caught her arm. 'It's true.

After we'd dropped you off on Friday, we went to fill up with petrol and we got done over at the garage. A gang of kids took both mine and Donovan's.' She made no reaction. Maybe he shouldn't have told her they were kids – now she might think he was a total wimp. 'They had knives and everything,' he added, hoping for the sympathy vote if nothing else.

He watched her hesitate as though weighing up the odds on what he'd said being true.

'And you couldn't find the time to come over and explain?'

'I was at my cousin's wedding in Brighton – I told you about it.'

'All weekend?'

'Yes – all weekend.' He held his breath – waiting. She had to believe him. He really liked her. Really, *really* liked her. 'Weddings are pretty big in my family.' Still no response. 'The Glastonbury Festival takes less organisation than a Khan family wedding.' He smiled, hoping that he could win her over with a joke.

'Oi! You!' A man's voice interrupted the interaction. 'Give us back my hat!'

'Oh, I'm sorry.' Zak held out the hard hat as the workman jumped down the final few rungs of the ladder from the scaffolding and snatched it off him.

'Vandalising other people's bleedin' skips and then nicking my hat. I could 'ave you for this.'

Zak bit back the reply he would've liked to have made but settled for a simple, 'Look, I've said I'm sorry – OK?'

But when he turned round, Mercedes had gone. A weight like a skipful of concrete descended on his shoulders. And, once inside the bank a notice on the door of the lift advising of essential maintenance work did little to improve his mood and he limped his way up to fourth floor. He would have to wait until lunchtime now and hope that he could catch her then. But as he rounded the corner into his office, the formidable figure of Sukhvinder Chadha awaited him.

'We do not operate a policy of flexitime, Zaki. You are well aware of the hours of your employment. Therefore you will make up the time you've lost at lunchtime.'

Brilliant! His day had just gone from totally crap to universally crappier!

It had not been Mercedes' intention to avoid Zak for the entire day; circumstances had just conspired that it should happen that way. She'd been at the point of accepting his explanation as to why he hadn't phoned her when she'd been shocked to see Gary, the man whom she and Jenny had seen in the café, doing a passable impersonation of Spiderman on the scaffolding. She thought it was a pretty safe bet that he wouldn't recognise her but she wasn't going to risk it. And anyway, she didn't want to be late on her first day. Darting into the bank before Gary could see her, she decided to catch up with Zak at lunch.

Her morning though had dragged by like a wet bank holiday. All she had done had been to sit behind a woman called Dilys who looked as though she'd stepped through a timewarp from the 1970s. Mercedes' morning had included such riveting activities as watching Dilys as she counted money, watching her as she'd stamped receipts and watching her as she'd added up columns of figures. By the time Dilys took her lunch break, Mercedes had been verging on a coma.

'Mrs Chadha told me I'd have a young girl shadowing me this week,' her mentor told Mercedes, gleefully unaware of the wince of irritation from Mercedes at being referred to as a 'young girl,' 'so I made extra sandwiches especially. I thought, as it's a nice day, we could go over to Green Park.'

Even if the lunch extravaganza of peanut butter and gherkin sandwiches had been a taste sensation that really appealed to Mercedes, the promised 'fizzy pop' accompaniment was not something that she was prepared to inflict on her digestive tract.

'Thanks, Dilys, but I've made other plans. I'll see you back at two thirty.'

But, just as any plans Mercedes might have made about finding Zak at lunchtime had been scuppered by Sukhvinder Chadha and her workplace detention, so any plans she might have had to try to catch him as he left work were scuppered by the fact that she was babysitting Alfie and Paige that night and had to leave on the dot of five.

As she left the bank she stood on the steps and took the sort of deep inhalation that comes with freedom. Never in her darkest moments of doubt about her placement had she envisaged tedium as mindnumbing as her first day. Then, before stepping out of the building, she did a quick recce of the scaffolding next door, checking for lurking work mates of her brother. She knew Chubby's firm were working on a site up West, but was it her unbelievable bad luck that it was bang next door to where she was working, or what?

She walked towards the Tube station, her eyes constantly on the look out for any sign of Zak. But to no avail.

What she did see, however, was much more irritating. A clamped Range Rover was being winched on to a low-loader ready to take it away to the pound. And there was something horribly familiar about the vehicle. It wasn't just the mud splattered sludge colour that reminded her of Chubby's car, or the rubber Homer Simpson figure that clung on to the windscreen with suction cups – but the registration plate was unmistakable: CHU 33 Y.

It was bad enough that half her family had unwittingly turned up to her first date *and* placed their spies on the building site next to her work placement, but now her brother was putting in an appearance on her first day at work as well! What the hell was going on in her life? Logically, she knew it must just be coincidence – no one had even asked where her work experience was – but she was still annoyed. And, irrational as it was, there was part of her that thought it served him right that he was getting towed away. She pushed her bowling bag high on to her shoulder and stamped angrily towards the Tube, abandoning her search for Zak. After all, if he'd really wanted to meet her, he'd have made the effort to come and find her, wouldn't he?

* * *

'Here you go, Merce. We're going over to Tone and Kelly's at Tilbury. This is their number, just in case.' Cheryl handed Mercedes a piece of paper. 'You know where everything is, help yourself.' She paused, cocking an ear towards the mahogany staircase and the heart-rending sobbing that was filtering through the mahogany panelled nursery door. 'Paige'll calm down after a bit. It's just that Frankie don't want her to have her security blanket and she's fretting. She'll be all right in a little while though.' It seemed that Cheryl was trying to convince herself more than Mercedes. 'And Alfie's to go to bed at half seven. D'you hear that Alfie?' she said, pointedly.

'Aw! Can't I stay up till eight?'

'Half seven!' Frankie entered the room, his face contorted with irritation.

'OK, Dad.' The five-year-old tucked his thumbs into the waistband of his pyjamas and left the kitchen with a gait worthy of a Wild West gunslinger.

'You OK, babes?' Cheryl asked her husband.

'No, I'm not flamin' OK!' he snapped. 'We'll have to take the Shogun tonight 'cos we're picking Chubby up on the way. Jeez!' He slammed his fist down on the marble effect kitchen counter. 'That brother of mine ain't got the brains 'e was bleedin' born with!'

112

Mercedes knew the cause of her brother's anger but she had decided that discretion was definitely her best policy.

'I don't mind taking the Shogun,' Cheryl appeased.

'Well I do!' He ran his fingers through his hair. 'I wanted to take the Porsche tonight.'

Cheryl raised her eyes skyward as she picked up her car keys. 'Later, Merce!' she called as she and Frankie left the house. 'And don't worry about Paige. She will settle – eventually.'

No way! Mercedes closed the door and went straight up to her niece's room. She'd had a bad enough day as it was, she wasn't going to have her evening disrupted too! And anyway, she couldn't bear to hear the toddler in such distress.

'Come on, darling.' Mercedes picked up the two year old and attempted to comfort her but Paige would have none of it. The little girl thrashed and kicked until there were the beginnings of a sizeable bruise on Mercedes' shoulder. When it was obvious that a simple cuddle was not working, Mercedes tried to soothe her with a drink of milk but the plastic bottle ricocheted off her head and bounced its way through the array of soft toys on top of the chest of drawers, knocking them over like skittles. Next she tried a lullaby, pacing the nursery floor singing anything she could recall from her own playgroup days. Sadly that only succeeded in cranking up Paige's howls until they reached a crescendo that could have split the atom. In desperation Mercedes took her downstairs and offered her a biscuit which went the way of all her other attempts to placate the child – straight in Mercedes' face.

By eight o'clock, Mercedes was splattered with a cocktail of milk, apple juice and soggy chocolate chip cookie with a hint of banana, whilst Paige had developed the decibel level of a foghorn and the complexion of an aubergine. Against Frankie's wishes, Alfie was still glued to his Playstation 2 – but, tough! If Frankie had wanted him in bed at seven thirty he should have made sure that Paige would settle first. And anyway, any grief from her brother and Mercedes could always play the Honey Coombes card – although she had been hoping to keep that up her sleeve for a little longer.

'Alfie, what does your mum do when Paige is like this?' she asked her nephew.

Without taking his eyes from the screen he replied, 'She gives her her blanket.'

'Yes,' she said, trying to remain as patient as she could. 'But your dad's thrown it away.'

'No he ain't. It's in his office.'

Mercedes could hardly believe her ears. 'So you've let your sister scream the place down for over an hour and you didn't tell me that the means of stopping her was only in another room?'

'No point,' he said, his thumbs moving across the buttons of the console like lightning. 'It's locked.'

Mercedes tried to put Paige on the floor but the child's screams reached new heights and she picked her up again. If Mercedes remembered correctly the lock on Frankie's office was a numbered security device and without the combination she had about as much chance of cracking the code as she did of winning the lottery.

'Alfie,' she called through to the lounge, 'do you know what numbers your dad presses to get in here?'

Alfie left his game and stood between Mercedes and the door from the hall to the office. 'Daddy don't let no one in his special room without him.'

'I know that, but Daddy doesn't let you stay up till eight o'clock either, does he?' she said, glaring at her nephew.

Alfie looked her straight in the eye, weighing up the situation, then pressed out a sequence of five dots on the wall next to his father's study.

'So, it's a five digit combination?' Mercedes looked at the ten number pads on the door. 'Well that lowers the odds a bit. I don't suppose you can remember any of the numbers, can you?'

Alfie shook his head. Mercedes jiggled the now hysterical Paige on her hip and sighed. She could be there all night trying to work out the combination.

'I only know the first and the last,' Alfie added.

OK – so now she only needed the middle three digits – that wasn't so bad. She was down to only about a million possibilities. 'So what are they?' she asked the five-year-old.

'The first one is a eight,' he said, pointing to the number eight. 'And the last one is a two.'

Mercedes gave a chuckle. 'And your daddy says Uncle Chubby doesn't have the brains he was born with!'

The twins had been born on the second of October nineteen seventy eight and it didn't take a genius to see that Frankie had simply reversed his date of birth for the combination. She quickly punched in the numbers eight, seven, zero, one, two and turned the knob. The door opened and Paige's screams were reduced to a whimper the second she spied her blanket in a heap on her father's leather-topped desk.

Mercedes turned to Alfie. 'OK – here's the deal. You can have an extra five minutes on your

Playstation and I won't say a word to Daddy if you won't. Done?' She held out her hand.

Alfie slapped it in a low five. 'Done,' he said and scurried back to the television to take up where he'd left off.

Her plan was to wait until Paige was asleep then take the blanket back and replace it. Frankie had an eye for detail that put many a bird of prey to shame, therefore it was crucial that she remember exactly where it was positioned. The bulk of it was crumpled up just to one side of the computer keyboard but one corner was tucked underneath a folder of papers. Still only having the use of one hand, she began to move the folder but the anticipation was too much for Paige who leant forwards and grabbed the piece of rag, knocking the folder on to the floor and scattering its contents.

'Sugar!' she sighed. Why was nothing simple? She was going to have to make certain that the papers went back in exactly the right order or it would be a dead giveaway.

Mercedes took the now peaceful two-year-old upstairs and tucked her up in bed. It would only be a matter of minutes before she was sound asleep. Once Alfie was also in bed she returned to the study to put back the blanket and tidy the papers. They'd fallen

117

in a neat fan shape, which meant the order was not disturbed, so at least something was going right.

But, on opening the folder, she was shocked to see that the top piece of paper was a hand-written note on a memo pad that she recognised instantly. It was one of the pale blue corporate note pads that were on every desk at work and had the Boreham's Bank logo in one corner and the word 'Memorandum' in the bank's corporate font across the top. The message was written in immature handwriting and had some dates and times which meant nothing to her:

Sid

Sun. Mon. Tues. 2 pm – 10 pm,

Wed. day off.

Thurs. Fri. Sat. – night duty. 10 PM – 6 AM.

She turned it face down and looked at the piece of paper beneath. The handwriting on this note was more mature and it read:

Spinks is going to roll the blag. Be careful, Jonnie 'Schizo' Sabatini is running the job.

She stared at it for some minutes trying to make sense of it all. Why should anyone be writing to tell her family that Harry Spinks was going to hijack a robbery? And she'd put money on the fact that, with a nickname like 'Schizo' this Sabatini guy wasn't going to be a social worker. She placed that one face down too, so that she could keep the papers in order and read the next letter. It was a print-out of an email from someone called Nicos Evangelides and said,

Merchandise arriving Saturday. Don't want to spoil the old lady's bash.

Will sort it with K & T.

Nicos Evangelides? Of course! The Mediterranean-looking man from the night club. It didn't take a linguistic genius to work out that Nicos Evangelides was Nick the Bubble whom she'd overheard Gary and the security guard talking about in the café. Bubble and squeak – Greek! And the merchandise must be the 'hardware' they'd mentioned. Things were starting to fit into place now. K & T – hadn't she heard them refer to Canvey Kev and Tilbury Tone? Which is where Frankie and Chubby had gone this evening – to Tone's in Tilbury. So, whatever it was, they really were all in on it – her entire family, including Cheryl.

She flicked on to the next paper; a list of phone numbers. The final documents in the folder were the bulkiest of all. There were three large pieces of paper that had been folded to an eighth their original size. Carefully she laid one of them out on the floor of the office and saw that it was an architect's drawing. The words 'basement level' were written in the bottom right-hand corner and 'Jimmy's Casino, St James's Square' was written at the bottom left-hand corner. These must be the plans to the building next to the bank that Zak had told her was being converted into a gaming club. But why would they be at Frankie's house when it was Chubby who ran the building side of the business? Trying to make sense of it all was like trying to piece together a jigsaw with no picture to go by. Carefully, she folded it up again and opened out the next drawing. She sat back on her heels and stared at the grey paper and the words that leapt out at her. There, in bold type, in the bottom left-hand corner were the words.

BOREHAM'S BANK, ST JAMES'S SQ. SW1

Oh dear God! She was aware that she'd stopped breathing. The alarm bells in her head were sounding the red alert. The pieces were falling into place and a horrible picture was beginning to emerge: the dodgy geezers who ran the Terra Firma, Spinks going to hijack the blag, Chubby the named driver, Nick the Bubble supplying the hardware! Try as she might to think of a legitimate explanation, the appalling reality was beginning to reveal itself like toxic waste appearing through a mushroom cloud of deceit.

Quickly she folded up the drawing and opened up the last one. Again, it was of the basement of the bank but this time showing the electrical circuits and alarm systems. Her worst fears were confirmed: her brothers were planning a robbery and it was at none other than the bank where she was working.

Eight

All these years Mercedes had thought that Harry Spinks and his dirty dealings had been the cause of her father's death: she'd assumed that he had somehow tried to extort money from the family firm and the stress had caused her dad's heart attack. At least, she'd prided herself, *her* family were honest upstanding citizens and weren't villains like the Spinks, who deserved all they got. But here, staring her in the face, was incontrovertible evidence to the contrary. This was just too awful.

And who else was privy to what appeared to be the underworld's worst-kept secret? She bit her lip nervously. Harry Spinks obviously knew, but what about his daughter? Was that what her mysterious comment the previous week had been about when she'd said that Mercedes' brothers wished Harry Spinks would go down? It was all starting to make horrible sense. And Uncle Horace's long absences – not, as Mercedes had gullibly thought, off making money on the oil fields of Kuwait but more than likely stirring porridge at Her Majesty's pleasure.

Now she came to think of it, she'd overheard her own father threatening to send someone down for a long stretch, just before he'd died.

A wave of fury enveloped her! How could they? She knew that, as far as school was concerned, she wasn't exactly Ms Goody-two-shoes herself but at least she only stretched the rules a bit and even when they got distorted totally out of shape, like running the sweepstakes, it was all in a good cause. But bank robbery! You weren't talking petty misdemeanours here; this was hard-core criminal activity! And at her bank too! *Her* bank! She felt ridiculously protective all of a sudden. Hadn't her brothers thought about *her* in all this? Had no one thought to mention the fact – oh by the way, sis, that work experience placement of yours is going to be done over! Although, if she really thought about it, no one had actually asked her *where* her placement was; she could've been behind the counter in their local NatWest for all they knew. Sitting round the breakfast table, having cosy family chats over the cornflakes had never been high on the Bent list of priorities.

The more she thought about it, the more angry she felt. This had all sorts of connotations. If they got caught (which must be at least an evens chance),

Mercedes herself couldn't help but be implicated. The Old Bill were sure to think that she'd got her placement there deliberately so that she could have access to inside information. And what about Zak? He'd be under suspicion too. What a nightmare! She'd have to stop seeing him. She'd have to leave the bank (although, despite her sudden burst of indignation at the thought of the robbery, that might definitely be a plus).

But the prospect of not seeing Zak again was the worst thing. Even if she met him coincidentally in the High Street she'd either have to avoid him forever or try to explain about her sudden departure. Everything was suddenly so complicated. It was going to require some serious brain pumping if she was going to find a way through this, and the first thing she needed to do was to cover her tracks and restore Frankie's office to the state it had been in before she went in there. She folded up the circuit plan, placed it at the back of the folder and put the folder back on the desk covering the edge of Paige's security blanket. Then she went to the kitchen, took one of the cloths from under the sink and wiped every surface she'd touched – just in case.

She shut the door just as the house phone rang.

'You all right, Merce?' It was Nanny Bent, back

from Spain the previous day, and she sounded concerned.

'Fine,' Mercedes replied, trying to steady the nervousness in her voice.

'Only you don't sound yourself, darlin'.'

'No, I'm fine, really. Paige was quite difficult to get off to sleep and I'm a bit tired after work, that's all.'

'Only some boy's been round 'ere asking after you.'

Some boy? Mercedes thought her heart would burst out of her rib cage it was beating so hard. 'What boy?'

'Let me get my glasses, darlin'.' There was a pause that seemed like a year while Nanny Molly scrabbled through her bag. 'Nice lad, 'e was. Left 'is new phone number. Said 'is old phone got half inched. 'Ere we are. Let's have a look – Zak. That's it. I knew it was something a bit different. 'E wanted to know where you was babysitting . . .'

'You didn't tell him, did you?' Mercedes cut in. She knew that Zak lived in the same road as her brother, the last thing she wanted was for him to turn up and recognise Frankie's house as that of the club owner.

'Course not, darlin'. What d'you think I'm like? 'E gave me his number, though. Do you want me to give it to you?'

125

There was a huge part of Mercedes that wanted his number as much as David Beckham wanted to play football and yet this couldn't be a worse time. 'Put it by the phone will you, Nan, and I'll get it when I get home.'

'You ain't half sounding out of sorts, love. Tell you what, I'll call meself a minicab and come round there, then you can come home and I'll stay and look after the nippers. How's that sound?'

It sounded like bliss. 'Thanks Nan, I could do with an early night.'

Once back home, Mercedes put Zak's new number straight into her phone and sent him a text message:

Meet me @ Starbucks @ 8.15 2moro mornin.

Now, she just had the knotty little problem of the robbery to sort out.

'I ain't going back there!' Harley Spinks threw her tennis racquet across the floodlit tennis court in the garden of her house in Chigwell, then kicked the ball in the same direction.

Her father removed his glasses and wiped his forehead wearily. 'Swede 'art, swede 'art . . .' His heavy London accent made the term 'sweetheart' sound more like Scandinavian painting-by-root-vegetable. 'I thought you *wanted* to do your work experience at the tennis club.'

'Well I don't!'

In any other circumstance, Harry Spinks was as hard as coffin nails but, around his only child, he became as malleable as Semtex. 'Darlin' – you only done one day. You gotta give these things a chance.'

'Well I ain't gonna!' She stared at her father, challenging him to disagree. 'I spent all poxy morning watching fat old biddies with bingo arms flirting with Sergio and then 'e expects me to go round picking up their balls. And then I was all afternoon in some poxy school running round picking up more balls for snotty nosed little brats.' She sent another tennis ball flying against the wire netting that surrounded the court. 'I ain't goin' back, Dad, and that's that!'

'Razor!' Harry sighed and called his dog over. 'Fetch, boy!' he said, pointing to the tennis balls.

Razor was another of Harry's weak spots. When, five years earlier, one of his enforcers had reported that a pub landlord was unable to come up with his 'insurance' payment that week but had offered Harry the pick of the litter from his prize Rottweiler in lieu, Harry had agreed. The then ten-year-old Harley had been wanting a pet for some time and this seemed too good an opportunity to miss; fulfilling his daughter's wishes and providing himself with a guard dog at the same time. What no one realised, however, was that the landlord's pedigree bitch, Roxy, had had an illicit rendezvous with Pierre the standard poodle from next door. As Razor grew it became increasingly obvious that the only features he'd inherited from Roxy had been her tan coat – and even that had been reduced to a peachy-beige when crossed with Pierre's curly white fur. But, like the Emperor's new clothes, no one ever mentioned the fact. Ever since Eric 'Hardman' Watson, now known as Eric 'Harmless' Watson, had referred to Razor as 'that strawberry blond teddy bear', the word on the street was that Razor was a Rottweiler – or else!

'Fetch it, go on! Fetch, boy!' Razor disappeared in the opposite direction and Harry walked over and picked up the two balls. 'You want me to talk to Sergio and get him to cancel 'is other clients? What do you want me to do about it, swede 'art? Just tell me.'

'I want a proper job.'

'You got a proper job, darlin'.'

'No – I've got the sort of job that morons do to earn pocket money. I want a job where I can wear proper clothes and work with proper people who don't have either flappy underarms or snivelling noses.'

Harry walked over to the electric ball-feeder machine and dropped the two tennis balls into the metal basket at the back. 'You gotta help me out here, darlin'. Tell me what you want and I'll sort it, OK?'

'I want a job like that Bent cow's got. She gets to go up West and everything.'

Harry Spinks stiffened at the mention of the name Bent. ' 'Ow long you two been mates then?'

Harley almost choked on the gum she was chewing. 'She ain't no flamin' mate of mine!' Her father seemed relieved. 'I said I wanted a job *like* hers: I didn't say I wanted to work *with* her.' She cocked her head on one side and adopted a look that was as near to wistful as she could manage. 'Cynthia says she's seen 'er on the Tube all tarted up like one of them computers what works in the city.'

'Commuters, swede 'art. The word's commuters.'

Harley put her trainer against the wire mesh of the tennis feeder and kicked it over, sending fifty balls rolling across the asphalt. 'I want you to sort me out a decent job not give me flamin' English lessons.'

Harry bent down and began picking up the balls. 'No need to get upset, swede 'art. Just tell me where she's working and I'll sort it.'

'I told you – I don't want to be where she is. She's

in some bank or other; Bashem's or Bonham's or something. I don't want to do nothing like that.'

Harry straightened up. 'You don't mean Boreham's?'

'Something like that but I've just said . . .'

'Hold on, darlin', hold on.' Harry's mind was in overdrive. So the Bent brothers were making this a family affair, were they? Obviously putting their little blister in there to get information. And from what he'd heard she'd got more brain cells than her two brothers put together – not that that was saying much. They were hardly the dynamic duo. In fact, since Big Al had died, Harry thought he could say, with some degree of confidence, that the Bents had never really challenged him for supremacy in East London. It'd been a good move, coming over the river. He'd never looked back. His empire ran the length of the District Line from Aldgate to East Ham and he had a finger in just about every pub, club, gym and snooker hall along the way.

Although he had to admit he was not well pleased that the Bents had gone into his manor and got their grubby little mitts on the Terra Firma. He was not pleased at all. That was a nice showcase that attracted punters from the literati and glitterati across London. Of course Tweedle Dum and

Tweedle Dumber went around lording it because they thought it gave them some sort of credibility amongst the toffs and boffs. As if! No, they should've stuck to their own patch.

After all, look how good he'd been to them. He could put his hand on his offshore bank balance and say in all honesty (well, when Harry said *honesty* he was meaning it to be taken in its broadest sense), that he'd been very respectful after Big Al had died. He'd dropped his bid to take over his old adversary's territory along the Central Line and had more or less allowed his boys a free rein. After all, Harry's dad, Gaffer Spinks, was old enough to remember the old days when gang warfare had all but ruined the profession. No one won in the end. So, Harry had been magnanimous towards the Bents; live and let live was his motto – within reason obviously; with maybe a little bit of maiming – just to keep people on their toes. Harry liked to think of it as his contribution to charity work.

But the Bent boys had overstepped the mark when they took over the Terra Firma. So, Harry had decided, as soon as he'd got the information on the Boreham's blag; no more Mr Nice-guy Spinks! In fact, he'd convinced himself, they deserved to get stitched up. They'd brought it on themselves – practically begging to be done over, they were. In fact, it would have been a crime to ignore their pleas.

Now, though, he was unsettled. The girl put a different complexion on things. Although, he mused, maybe they'd got a point. The Gaffer had trained Harry up as soon as he was into long trousers so why shouldn't the Bents bring their little sister in on the job? Harry looked across the tennis court to where his own daughter was glowering at him with a face like a volcano on the point of eruption. He knew he was a bit overprotective with her sometimes, so maybe it would do her good to start working for the firm.

He smiled, fondly. 'Tell you what, darlin', 'ow d'you fancy learning the ropes with your old dad?'

'Work with *you*?' Harley looked as though she would be sick any moment.

'No, no, no. Not, strictly speaking, *with* me.' Even Harry could see that that might stretch his paternal instincts to the limit. 'With Rita. Up at the office in Wardour Street.'

His daughter paused, suspiciously. 'Doing what?'

'Personnel management.'

Harley looked more interested.

'Rita's my right-hand woman; gives the lads their work, keeps tabs on things, goes round and does spot checks – that sort of thing. You could get an overview of the business.'

There was a short silence while she weighed up the situation. 'Do I get to wear proper business clothes?'

'Course you do, swede 'art. I'll get Rita to take you out tomorrow and buy you whatever you want.'

'And do I get to go on the Tube? I don't want you driving me up there.'

'Course, darlin'.'

'But I want you to drive me to Snaresbrook station. I don't want to go from here. The cow might not see me, if I go from here.'

'No problem, princess.' Harry put his arm round his daughter's shoulders and they walked back towards the house together.

'And,' Harley said, 'I don't want to have tennis lessons any more.'

'You don't have to, my angel.'

'And I want Sergio sacked from the club. He had no right to treat me that way.'

Harry sighed, heavily. 'Course 'e didn't, my precious.'

But even Harry had to admit that sacking seemed a bit steep. He'd have a word with Sergio tomorrow and just ask him to keep a low profile for a few weeks. If past form was anything to go on, Harley would change her mind in about a week's time. Meanwhile, he'd let her settle in with Rita for a couple of days and then work on building a friendship between her and the Bent girl: see what information she could wheedle out of her about the blag.

Frankie cupped his brandy glass and swilled the contents round with mesmerising menace. Cheryl, Kelly and Kev's girlfriend, Leonie, had left the room but Frankie still seemed irritated by their distant laughter as it drifted through from the kitchen. The four men; himself, Chubby, Tone and Kev, stared at the crumb-strewn table and what remained of Tone's thirtieth birthday cake.

Without taking his eyes from the circling liquid Frankie spoke. 'You put us in a very dodgy situation today, bruv. Very dodgy.'

'It was an emergency, Frankie, honest.'

Silence pervaded the dinner table. It was as though, when the women had left, the detonator had been pressed and the other three men were simply waiting for the explosion.

'A new building inspector'd turned up and Gary didn't know . . .' Chubby continued.

'Whose name is on the deeds, Chub?' Frankie interrupted quietly.

'James Squires,' his brother answered meekly.

'And who is James Squires?'

' 'E don't exist except on paper.'

'And why is that, bruv?'

'So 'e can't be traced.'

Frankie took a slug of the spirit and placed his glass on the table. He looked round the faces and nodded slowly. 'So far, so good. Now, who's doing the conversion work for our non-existent Mr James Squires?'

'ABC Limited, bruv.'

Frankie nodded again. 'I know you wasn't exactly Einstein at school, Chubs, but just humour me on this and try to remember what ABC stands for.'

Chubby sighed. 'Anonymous Building Contractors.'

'And that would be because?'

'Because we don't want anything what could link Bent Enterprises with the blag.'

'So,' Frankie took another swig of his brandy, 'maybe you could explain to me and the lads why, when we're bustin' a gut to keep our 'eads down, you go swanning in there like Father flippin' Christmas, handing them evidence like spending

135

time in the clink was the next best thing to a weekend at the Ritz?'

Chubby slumped in his chair. 'Look, I know I was a bit stupid—'

'Stupid? Stupid don't even come close to you, bruv.' Frankie banged his hand on the table. 'Stupid would get the Nobel Prize for intelligence compared to you! Jeez, I don't think I know anyone what's as intellectually challenged as you, Chubby! You are a flamin' liability, that's what you are. Three flamin' months we been planning this blag and you put the whole bleedin' job in jeopardy 'cos a new building inspector turns up and Gary panics.'

'Give 'im a break, Frank,' Tone cautioned.

Frankie stood up and walked round the table until he was standing behind his brother. 'Give 'im a break? I'll give 'im a flamin' break.' He put his hands on his brother's shoulders. 'I'll break 'is flamin' neck if this job don't come off 'cos of 'im.'

He returned to his place and reached into his inside pocket. The others ducked down with timing worthy of a synchronised swimming team then, in unison, breathed a sigh of relief when Frankie produced a cigar rather than the handgun they had been half expecting.

'From now on,' he continued, rolling the cigar

between his fingers. 'I don't want you nowhere near the site, do you understand?'

'Yes, Frankie.'

'And that includes you being off the job.'

'Aw, Frankie.'

'This is non-negotiable, Chubby. You're a known face what's got 'imself nicked not four hundred yards from a bank what's going to get done over. From now on, I want you as far out of the way as possible. Go to Tenerife, Timbuktu, Tasmania, anywhere but you do not set foot within ten miles of the West End, am I making myself clear?'

Chubby nodded sadly. He'd only been trying to help. Gary had rung him in a right state because the new inspector had turned up unannounced and been asking questions about the hole that was being cut through into next-door's basement. The plan had been to remove all the plaster and most of the bricks at the casino side of the wall, leaving only a thin layer at the bank side which could be easily broken through on the night of the blag. Each evening at knocking-off time, the hole would be covered up with sheets of Gyproc plasterboard to conceal the fact that there was an opening big enough for a small army. Normally, they had warning of an inspection but that afternoon had taken everyone by surprise. Chubby had dropped everything (including five litres of cardinal-red paint on the freshly polished parquet floor of the site they were just finishing in Docklands), to dash to St James's Square and try to placate the building inspector. When he'd arrived he'd been astounded to find that the person who'd got Gary's knickers in a knot had been a woman.

'Myrtle Monk.' She'd held out her hand to shake Chubby's and, as she did so, dropped her briefcase.

'Let me,' Chubby had offered, finding himself unexpectedly smiling at the council officer. Straightening up he handed her back her briefcase and took her hand. 'Ch—' He'd stopped himself. 'Charles,' he corrected. 'Charles Bent. Pleased to meet you.'

She must have been at least ten years his senior but there was something inexplicably attractive about her. Not only had Chubby never had a girlfriend, but he'd never even dared to dream that one day he might have one. However, in the millisecond that his eyes had met hers, Myrtle had become the object of his desire. He had been struck by her warm smile and friendly approach. ('Friendly as a bleedin' werewolf,' Gary had commented.) And her name; Myrtle – he loved it; he'd once had a terrapin called Myrtle the Turtle when he was younger and the inspector's presence was bringing back fond memories.

'Let me show you the site, Miss Monk,' he'd offered, keen to get her as far away from the basement as possible. 'Or, may I call you Myrtle?' Chubby hadn't watched his brother flirting for the past twelve years without picking up a few tips.

She'd readily accepted his explanation that the brickwork had been damaged by flooding and needed replacing, based entirely on Chubby's own testimony that flood damage didn't need to come from an external source. He had guided her around the site having only one momentary difficulty when he had stepped on the unsecured end of a scaffold plank and catapulted a bucket of plaster over the banisters of the fifth floor so that the central stairwell and every workman within spillage distance had been splattered with the gloopy pink mixture. Myrtle, unlike his employees, appeared not to have noticed. She seemed to be as enamoured of Chubby as he was of her and she departed having given Chubby her phone number and invited him to call her. Chubby had been left feeling warm and fuzzy inside which had lasted as long as it took him to walk round the corner and see the space at the side of the road where his Range Rover had been parked.

He drew his attention back to where Frankie was delivering the revised plan.

' 'Orace will be the first driver. He's experienced and 'e knows the ropes.'

'I thought, 'cos 'Orace had only just come out, 'e wanted to stay clean for a bit,' Tone commented.

' 'E did but Brain of Britain over there put paid to that.'

Chubby made no comment. He'd have liked to have gone home there and then but he was relying on Frankie for a lift.

'And, Kev, you'll be the second driver, orright?'

Kev nodded, trying not to let Chubby see the smirk that was spreading across his lips.

'So, we got ten days to go. I don't want no one getting into any bother, right? No speeding tickets, no nicking, no handling. We keep our noses clean from now till the off. Is that understood?'

'Sure,' Tone nodded.

Chubby said nothing.

Kev grinned cockily. 'Or else?'

Frankie turned on him. 'You don't wanna know the answer to that, Kev my old sunshine.' He took Kev's cheek between his fingers and pulled it hard. 'And you know what they say; if you don't wanna know the answer, don't ask the flamin' question.'

'Just 'aving a laugh, Frankie. Just pulling your old mystic. No offence meant.'

Frankie patted Kev's face and smiled. 'And none taken, mate.' He straightened up. 'Right, Nick the Bubble's delivering the gear to the lock-up next Saturday so we'll have a meet at Kev's on Sunday. I'll see you then. Come on, Chub. I want to go home. I'm cream crackered.'

'Cheers, Tone. Happy birthday, mate.' Chubby mustered a smile as they left. The departure could not come too soon for him. Had it not been for meeting Myrtle, today would have counted as one of his worst on record. He wondered if he should give her a ring when he got home, or was that too soon? Maybe he should leave it till tomorrow? It was so difficult. He'd never asked anyone out before. If Merce was still awake when Frankie dropped him off, he'd ask her how to go about it.

At precisely eight fifteen the next morning, Mercedes walked through the door of Starbuck's. Zak had already been there for ten minutes. His beam of recognition did not escape her and she went straight to his table without ordering coffee.

'Hi.' He reached out and took her hand in his. 'I looked for you all over yesterday . . .'

'Zak,' Mercedes said, softly. 'I asked you to meet me for a reason.' She bit her bottom lip nervously. The words felt heavy in her chest but she wanted to come straight to the point. No sense in beating about the bush and dragging things out. She took a deep breath and pulled her hand away. 'I can't see you any more.'

The smile slipped from Zak's face and he sat, shell-shocked for a moment. 'But—'

'I'm sorry,' she said. 'I'm really sorry.' God! If he knew what an understatement that was! One day she'd make her brothers pay for this.

'Why? I don't understand! I thought you had a good time on Friday.'

'I did.'

Zak leaned forward, annoyed. 'Jeez, Mercedes! Is this just because I didn't phone you at the weekend?'

Did he really think she was that petty? Mercedes folded her arms and looked away. 'No.'

Zak flung himself against the back of the chair and reached his arms out in a gesture of non-comprehension. 'Oh, pul-ease! I thought you were more mature than that.'

She raised her chin and narrowed her eyes in irritation. Mature? He didn't know the half of it. But she wasn't going to get drawn into explaining. 'It's got nothing to do with that.'

This was so much harder than she'd imagined it would be when she'd been lying in bed running through every possible alternative. Seeing him there in front of her she realised just how much she liked him. And she was dumping him because of her wretched family! Was this what the rest of her life was going to be like? Never getting close to boys in case they found out about her background? She ran through an imaginary introduction; 'Hi, my name's Steve and my family's in banking.' 'Pleased to meet you, I'm Mercedes and mine is too!' 'Really? High Street, or investment?' 'Robberies, actually.' Great chat-up lines of the century – not!

'I was telling the truth, you know – about my phone and the wedding and everything. You can ask Donovan.'

'I don't need to ask Donovan; I believe you.'

'So what is it then?' He stared at her across his latte. 'Come on, Mercedes, you've got to give me something to go on here.' He leaned forward again and lowered his voice. 'You can't kiss me the way you did on Friday and then suddenly say, that's all folks – see ya! That meant something to me, you know.'

Did he really think it hadn't meant anything to her? Mercedes could hardly bear it. She lowered her eyes and said nothing.

'Well, excuse me for misreading the messages, but I thought you liked me!'

'I did,' she said. Then added quietly, 'I do.'

It was Zak's turn to narrow his eyes – this time in concentration as though trying to solve some mathematical equation. There was something here that didn't add up. 'So why are you dumping me?'

'Believe me, it's better that we don't take this any further.'

'Better for whom? Not for me.' He watched her eyes, normally bright and sparkling but today they were flat and, unless his intuition had totally deserted him, there was pain there too. He reached out for her hand again but she pulled it away. 'And by the expression on your face, it's not better for you either, so something's going on here that I don't know about.'

Mercedes wanted to take a deep breath and tell him everything. It would be such a relief to be able to share this with someone, but how could she? He'd want her to go to the police and then what? Watch her entire family get locked up? Oh, sure, Frankie would survive in the nick and her mother would probably end up running Holloway Holistic Health from her cell, but Chubby? No way could she do that to Chubby.

'I'm right, aren't I?' Zak persisted.

Mercedes sighed. 'Please – you have to trust me on this.'

'Why?'

She straightened up and held his gaze. 'Because I'm asking you to.'

She had spent most of the previous night working out the outcomes to the various scenarios: if she went to the police now, she was certain that she could save herself and Zak but her family would go down for a very long time and they'd probably disown her for an even longer time. On the other hand, if she said nothing and let the robbery go ahead as planned, there was a strong possibility that her family would still go down and, simply because they were in the wrong place at the wrong time, she and Zak would be pursuing their relationship by correspondence from their respective detention centres. A third option, to confront Frankie and Chubby, wasn't even worth contemplating in terms of any long-term changes. They'd simply alter the date or the venue.

No, Mercedes realised that she was going to have to take the biggest gamble of her life. She was going to have to sacrifice her relationship with Zak before it had even had a chance to get off the ground, and do what the police would probably suspect her of doing anyway; she was going to be an insider. Only she was going to use whatever information she could glean to stop the blag without anyone knowing about it. If she pulled this off she'd save her family. If she didn't manage it, they'd all end up with a criminal record, herself included. Either way, Zak didn't and couldn't feature in her immediate future. She only hoped that, if their paths did cross in years to come, they could make a fresh start.

She pushed her bowling bag on to her shoulder and stood up. 'Bye, Zak.' She turned towards the door then stopped and faced him. 'That kiss meant a lot to me too.' With that, she left.

Nine

By the following Friday, Mercedes had just about reached the end of her tether. She had focused her attention on foiling the robbery and thought about little else for the entire week and yet she still hadn't the faintest idea how she was going to go about it. Her attempts to pump Dilys for information about the bank security systems had yielded little more than she could have gained from watching a promotional video for potential investors.

All she had managed to find out was that the bank vault was situated in the basement (which she knew from the architects' drawings) and was encased in reinforced steel and concrete that could withstand even a nuclear attack. (She knew that Frankie could get you almost anything you wanted but she was sure that not even he could lay his hands on the plutonium needed for that.) The security station was directly opposite the vault, so that the door was guarded at all times by at least one security guard and it could only be opened by two people simultaneously. Inside were not only the bank's cash reserves, but also several hundred safety deposit boxes which, like the door itself, required two people to open each one. If she hadn't seen the plans with her own eyes she would have offered a hundred to one on that it was impregnable.

Her mind was like a hamster on a caffeine-fest, manically running round and round and getting nowhere. The only consolation was that as long as she was occupied with the project she'd set herself, she wasn't thinking of Zak – or at least that was the theory. In reality, it hurt like hell to know that she was in the same vicinity as he was, let alone the same building. At first, he'd bombarded her with voicemail and text messages but as the week had progressed so, it appeared, had Zak's indifference. She had to admit that hurt a bit but, on the bright side, at least it proved she'd made the right decision and at work she made a point of avoiding the fourth floor and the staff cafeteria as though they'd been contaminated with anthrax.

By the time she got home at the end of her first week of work experience, she was tired, frustrated and her body felt as though it was lead-lined. All she wanted was a peaceful swim to try to wash away some of her stress but, as she switched on the kettle and looked out into the garden, she realised that there was fat chance of that. People and chairs and balloons littered the garden, not to mention the acre upon acre of canvas festooning the lawn in preparation for tomorrow's festivities. Great!

Her phone rang and she snapped it off without even checking to see who it was. She wasn't in the mood to speak to anyone – and it wasn't just Zak she wanted to shut out either; it was Jenny too. Donovan had taken Jenny out again on the Tuesday – the very same day Mercedes had told Zak that she wasn't going to see him any more. And Jenny, not being the most sensitive of people, hadn't stopped going on about it. Of course, Mercedes didn't like to think that she could ever be jealous of Jenny but she had to confess, her friend's newfound relationship was beginning to gall her.

No sooner had she switched off her mobile than the house phone began ringing. Mercedes ignored it. She'd lay fifty to one that it was the same person and she was no more inclined to talk now than she had been thirty seconds ago. A few minutes later Nanny Molly wandered in with the handset from the hall.

'Merce, babes, it's your mate, Jenny.'

'Cheers, Nan,' Mercedes said, somewhat sarcastically. Surely Nan could have worked out that if she'd wanted to speak to anyone she would have picked up the extension in the kitchen.

'You've got to help me out here,' Jenny burst out as soon as Mercedes spoke. 'I've got another date with Donovan and I'm having a clothing crisis. I need to borrow something for tomorrow.'

Mercedes felt irrationally ratty. 'Jen, you don't even know what a clothing crisis is. Mozambique is having a clothing crisis; Sudan has a clothing crisis. If you've got a clothing crisis, ring Oxfam.'

'Oooo! That's a bit harsh,' Jenny replied, obviously hurt. 'Honestly, I don't know what's eating you this week. I thought you'd be happy once you found out that Zak wasn't ignoring you, but he's told Donovan that you won't even speak to him. And you didn't return any of my calls yesterday. And now you're like a cow with a sore head just because I ask to borrow an outfit.'

'Bear,' Mercedes corrected. 'The expression is, a bear with a sore head.'

There was a momentary silence before Jenny said, 'I'm not a total plank you know, Mercedes. I knew what I meant to say.'

Mercedes felt a pang of guilt. She'd never heard Jenny so assertive and she realised that she'd been so wrapped up in her own difficulties that she'd lost sight of their friendship.

'I'm sorry, Jen. It's just that so much is going on here with the party and everything and I'm having a really crap time at work . . .' Even as she said the words, she knew that her excuses sounded hollow. The truth was that she was terrified out of her mind about the bank robbery and gutted beyond reason about Zak but she couldn't tell Jenny about either problem.

'Do you want to talk about it?' Jenny offered.

'No. I'll be fine. Everything'll be back to normal in just over a week.' She sighed: if only! Nothing would ever be the same again now that she knew the truth about her family.

'Well, can I come over and borrow something of yours, anyway?' Jenny persisted.

'Jen, it really isn't a good time here. We're swarming with blokes putting up the marquee and there's caterers coming out of the woodwork. And the way my mum's flapping around, she makes a headless chicken seem like a Buddhist on a meditation retreat. Anyway, I was just going to take the dogs out.'

'Great – I can meet you over at the café and you can bring something for me to wear tomorrow.'

Mercedes was just about to protest when Jenny fed her the line that had her hooked.

'And I'll fill you in on all the goss about Harley Spinks.'

'What about Har—?' she paused as her mother clicked by on her kitten-heeled slippers, screaming into her mobile.

'It ain't big enough. No way. I told you lot last week, I got two hundred for a sit-down and then we got a disco and a Queen tribute band. What d'you do, nick it from a bleedin' scout camp or something?' As Laverne passed her daughter she forced a grin and mouthed, 'Orright, babes?' before continuing with her tirade. 'Listen mate, I don't give a monkey's. Just sort it, orright!'

Mercedes returned to Jenny. 'OK. Where's he taking you?' she asked, reluctantly.

Jenny giggled. 'Can't tell you.'

Mercedes wasn't in the mood for games. She sighed, impatiently. 'How about my embroidered jeans and Ted Baker top and I'll see you over the caff in about twenty minutes?'

Mercedes waited while Jenny held the clothes up in front of her and did a twirl round the café.

'You're itching to know where we're going, aren't you?' Jenny teased.

'Not really – I'm just waiting for you to spill the beans on our pebbled-dashed friend.'

Jenny pushed the clothes back into the carrier and sat down. 'OK, get this; when Fern was going to work yesterday morning she saw Harley Spinks hanging around by the steps at Snaresbrook station and she was all dressed up in a business suit. Apparently she looked like a cross between an undertaker and a prison warder.'

Mercedes shuddered at the reference to prison warders. 'And? I don't get what's the hot goss about that.'

'Well,' Jenny continued, unable to conceal her excitement. 'Apparently she's not doing her work experience at the tennis club any more. In fact, she told Fern that she's given up tennis, so you might be in with a chance of winning the tennis cup when we go back. Isn't that brilliant?'

The tennis cup! Mercedes smiled at the irony; she'd been so wrapped up in trying to keep herself and her family out of prison that the school tennis cup seemed about a million light years away. 'Yes, brilliant.'

'But wait for this,' Jenny could barely contain herself. 'She told Fern that she's working with her dad now. So you know what that means?'

Mercedes knew only too well what it meant but she wanted to find out Jenny's interpretation first. 'No.'

'Oh, come on! It means that we were right about her all along. If her dad's the big-time criminal everyone makes him out to be and Harley's going to work for him, then it means she really is the lowest lowlife in the entire history of low-living!'

Mercedes shuffled uncomfortably. 'We shouldn't judge other people, Jen. My nan's got this old record by some woman called Joan Baez and there's a song on it called, "There but for fortune".'

Jenny looked bemused. 'Huh?'

'Think about it.'

'Honestly, Mercedes, what's got into you since you started work at that bank? You've been acting really weird all week. Have you caught religion or something?'

Just then Mercedes caught sight of a face she recognised at the door of the café. She kicked Jenny indicating for her to keep quiet and look nonchalant.

'Two teas please, Jase.' It was Gary, the man from the building site. 'And a bacon sarnie.' He went back to the door and shouted towards the small car park, 'You want a bacon sarnie with yours, Sid?'

Sid – that was the name Mercedes had seen written on the piece of paper in Frankie's study with a list of times below it. The second man appeared in his security guard uniform and this time he had his

'You should learn to keep your trap shut, Gary.'

'Stop getting your Y-fronts in a whirl – Jason's a safe geezer, you know that.'

'The sooner you learn that no one's safe the better. And anyway, you ain't the one what's in for a battering.'

Mercedes ears pricked up.

'Gordon Bennet, Sid! Enough of the bleedin' 'eart. It ain't like you're not getting paid. Your cut's at least three times what I'm getting.'

'Well for one thing that's 'cos I've got invaluable knowledge what they need, right? And for another – it ain't worth it.'

'You know your problem, mate? You don't know when you're on to a winner. You get roughed up a bit, a few days being waited on by some pretty young nurses, maybe even some compensation from the bank and then Bob's your uncle: all back to normal and enough dosh to take the missus to see your nipper down under.'

So that was it! Sid was the insider. He was the security guard at the bank, that must be what the list of times was in Frankie's folder; his shifts on duty. Sid was going to be the one who got the gang in but it needed to look as though he'd put up some resistance, so they were going to have to knock him about a bit to make it look genuine. Mercedes leaned forwards on her chair and folded her arms. She was furious! Not only were her brothers planning to steal other people's money but now, she discovered, someone was getting hurt in the process. And not just in an accidental, 'Oops, sorry mate – didn't mean to bash your head in' kind of way either. This was all premeditated.

'Cheers, Jase,' Gary said as Jason brought the men's food across.

While he was there, he leaned across and spoke to Mercedes. 'You all right there, Mer—' Mercedes glowered at him and shook her head, almost imperceptibly. 'Mer . . . my darlings.' Jason corrected himself.

Mercedes gave Jenny's leg a kick and indicated that Jenny should be the one to respond.

Jenny looked quizzically at her friend. 'Erm, yes, I think so. Aren't we?' she asked Mercedes.

Mercedes sighed and nodded. How on earth was she supposed to do undercover work with a sidekick like Jenny?

'What's going on?' Jenny whispered when Jason had gone.

Mercedes shrugged. 'I'm not sure, but I think it's best if you don't know.' Which wasn't entirely a lie.

'You heard that Chubby's off the job?' Gary said through a mouthful of bacon sandwich.

Mercedes was alert again and she leaned back to hear more.

'That don't surprise me,' replied Sid. 'So who's the driver then?'

' 'Orace.'

Sid almost choked on his gut-buster. 'Blimey! That should improve their . . . I mean *our* chances a bit then. So apart from that it's all sweet for next Friday?'

'Yeah.'

'You going to the meet Sunday?'

'Compulsory, mate. Compulsory.'

The two men chuckled and carried on eating their food. Mercedes was half relieved that Chubby was off the role of driver but also upset that they seemed to be casting aspersions on her brother's ability. She was feeling restless and if it hadn't been for the fact that she wanted to find out as much as she could about the robbery, she would have left.

'Hey, d'you hear he's got a girlfriend?' Gary laughed.

'What, Chubby? No way!'

Jenny's eyes widened and she was about to express her surprise when Mercedes gave her a look that would have silenced a lion mid-roar.

So that was what he'd been on about. Three times that week he'd tried to prise information out of her about how she would like to be treated by a boy. 'If you'd given somebody your number do you think it'd be OK to phone them the next day, or leave it a bit?' he'd asked her. And then, 'Merce, do you think blokes should buy women flowers, or is it a bit nerdy?' 'Hey, sis, let's say, just for instance, that you fancied this boy, right . . .' Finally, thinking that her nan must have told Chubby about Zak and he was winding her up, she'd almost bitten off his head. 'Get off my case, will you! My love-life has nothing to do with you or anyone else in this family!' Poor Chubby. She'd wondered why he'd looked like Genghis when Laverne had accidentally pierced his tail with her stiletto as a puppy. She made a mental note to talk to him when she got home.

She focused her attention on the conversation behind her again.

'Too right!' Gary went on between mouthfuls. 'It's this old bird what works for the council and he ain't half got the hots for her.'

Both men sniggered and Mercedes was incensed. She needed to get out of there before she leapt to her brother's defence and totally blew her cover. She would have preferred it if she'd been able to suss out the time and venue for the meet but she'd heard enough for one day.

Outside, Jenny had one last shot at probing her for information. 'What is this all about? Is Chubby in some sort of trouble?'

'I don't want to talk about it.'

Jenny sighed. 'Oh well, I'll see you tomorrow then.'

'No you won't, Jen – remember? It's Nan's party and I'm going to be helping in the morning and then the whole thing kicks off at three.'

'Oops!' Jenny squealed excitedly. 'I know – I'm coming.'

Mercedes felt sick. 'What?'

'When I rang up tonight, your nan answered and she invited me.' Jenny grinned. 'Donovan had suggested that we go out on Saturday anyway, so I thought – let's kill two birds with one stone. I was going to make it a surprise but you know me and secrets; I'm hopeless.'

This was awful. Jenny already knew Chubby and, much to Mercedes amazement, had accepted her explanation that Chubby's presence at the Terra Firma the previous week had been purely social: Donovan's brother must have made a mistake in identifying him as one of the owners. If she came to the party though, she couldn't help but recognise

160

Frankie and Uncle Horace as well. Coupled with the conversations she'd overheard and even with Jenny's lack of mathematical ability, she couldn't help but put two and two together and come up with something roughly between three and five.

'No!' Mercedes said, rather more sharply than she'd intended. 'I mean, it's supposed to be family only.'

'Well, try telling your nan that!' Jenny said, obviously put out. 'She's invited me and told me to bring some friends along too.'

This whole business was turning into an even worse nightmare than Mercedes could possibly have imagined. If Donovan went, he'd be bound to recognise her brothers and then he'd tell Zak and the whole thing would be out in the open. She had to stop Jenny turning up at all costs.

'Believe me, Jen you don't want to be there. It'll be really crap with a load of old fossils gassing away about the good old days. Really, it won't be worth it. You'd be better off going to the cinema or something.'

'Really?' Jenny cocked her head on one side. 'That's interesting, because your nan told me that there was going to be a hog roast in the afternoon with a juggler and fire-eater and then a sit-down meal in the evening followed by a disco and Freddy Mercury look-a-like.'

jacket over his shoulder with the Boreham's bank logo clearly visible. Mercedes stared at the floor, desperate not to be seen.

'Let's have a look.' He read from the large menu that was painted on the wall. 'Nah! I think I'll have a gut-buster,' he said, referring to the sausage, bacon, burger and egg sandwich that was named so descriptively.

'What you doing, stocking up to prepare yourself for a long stint in hospital?' Gary laughed. 'You're gonna be getting your guts busted well enough without that.'

'Leave it out.' Sid seemed irritated by the other man's joke.

'Only winding you up, mate.'

'Well don't.'

'What's this, Sid? You in for a spell with the old Nasty Health Service,' Jason asked as he flipped two rashers of bacon, a sausage and a beefburger on to the griddle behind the counter.

'Nah! Gary's just 'aving a laugh, ain't you, Gaz?' Sid glared at his mate as he said the words through gritted teeth.

The two men took their teas and sat at the table behind the girls while they waited for their food. Mercedes leant backwards in an attempt to listen in to their conversation.

Sugar! Since when had Nanny Bent believed that honesty was the best policy?

'Still,' Jenny went on, 'nice to know who my friends are, isn't it?' She pushed the carrier bag of clothes at Mercedes. 'I don't think I'd have felt right wearing your clothes to a party at your house, anyway.' And with that, she turned towards Whipps Cross Road and home.

Mercedes untied the dogs and walked off in the opposite direction. What on earth was happening to her life? She'd found and lost the most fantastic boy she'd ever met, discovered that everything she'd believed about her family was built on deception, upset Chubby and now she'd alienated her best friend. Meanwhile, back at the poolside, the Bent matriarchy were frenetically orbiting Planet Party, unaware that their future freedom lay in Mercedes' hands. She picked up a large lump of wood and hurled it angrily across the rough grassland behind the café. As she watched Attila and Genghis bound after it, she folded her arms and wondered if, by this time next week, she'd have *anyone* left in her life.

Ten

Zak drummed his fingers on the top of the steering wheel then dropped his head forward so that it rested between his hands. 'I'm not sure this is such a good idea.' The Beetle was parked on Honey Drive but, because the private road resembled the overcrowded forecourt of a four-wheel drive distributor, it was about five hundred yards from the Bent house.

'Course it is – it's brilliant,' Jenny reassured him from the passenger seat. She turned to the back of the car. 'Isn't it, Donovan?'

Donovan shrugged. 'I can see why you'd want me on your side but, sorry – I'm with Zak on this one. I'm thinking – if she was at all interested, she'd have rung him but the fact that she hasn't means she isn't! It doesn't need an agony aunt to work that one out.'

'Cheers, Dono!' Zak said, sarcastically. 'Way to boost my confidence!'

'No worries, mate.'

'Honestly! Why don't you believe me?' Jenny sighed and opened the car door regardless of her companions' reluctance. 'She *is* interested. Trust me.

And what's the worst that could happen anyway? She could refuse to see you and never speak to you again but, as that's already happened, so what?'

Zak took the keys out of the ignition and nodded. 'True.'

'Great! Come on.'

As the three of them approached the house they couldn't fail to notice the music growing louder and louder until, by the time they reached the gate, it had reached a level worthy of the fairground on Wanstead Flats. Billows of smoke rose from behind the house and the smell of roasting meat permeated the sticky afternoon air.

Donovan surveyed the driveway with dismay. 'Jeez, man! They're going to need to raise all the low bridges around here if these four wheel drives get any higher. It's like the Inspector Gadget car convention.'

Zak smiled nervously but Jenny seemed oblivious to anything other than her purpose for the afternoon. 'You see, I don't think that this has got anything to do with you, Zak. I've known her since we were eight years old and believe me, I know when something's not right. And I also know that Mercedes is the last person in the world to ask for any help. So, look on this as a mercy mission; you've come along to rescue a damsel in distress.'

Zak eyed Jenny incredulously. He may not have known Mercedes as long as she had but he was pretty certain that Mercedes was about as far removed from being a damsel in distress as he was from being Buzz Lightyear. He'd been about to argue the point when one of the hundred or so helium balloons that had been tied together to form a glittering tunnel up to the door, broke loose and drifted in front of him, momentarily startling him.

'Just chill, mate,' Donovan advised. 'You're jumpier than a kangaroo on a pogo stick.'

Easy for Donovan to say: he was already assured of Jenny's affection. Zak, on the other hand, hadn't a clue where he stood with Mercedes and that had never happened to him before. Ever since he'd pulled Carmen McParton at the school disco when he was fourteen, he'd been able to go out with any girl he'd wanted – until now. He was finding it very unnerving. And almost as unnerving was the fact that when they reached the front door, they were confronted by two bouncers whose bulky frames all but filled the space in the cavernous vestibule. One bouncer stepped forward and asked to see their invitations.

Jenny smiled easily. 'Oh, we haven't got invitations. We're friends of Mercedes and her nan only invited us on Thursday.'

The man spoke into his walkie-talkie checking out the validity of what Jenny had said but, while he was waiting for a response, the other heavy leaned forward and spoke to Donovan.

'Here, you ain't got a brother what's a DJ, have you?'

Donovan looked shocked. 'Yeah,' he answered, hesitantly.

'Gor – you don't half look like him an' all,' the bouncer grinned. 'He works down the club where we work. Here,' he said to the other doorman, 'this is Dylan's bro. Peas in a pod, or what?' After a brief discussion as to the family likeness between Dylan and Donovan, the group were waved into the house.

'What a coincidence,' Jenny said as they walked through the hall, towards the kitchen. 'How many clubs does your brother work at?'

'Just the one,' Donovan replied.

'Really?' Jenny continued. 'Wow! I wonder what odds Mercedes would give that? Your brother working at the club where Mercedes' nan hired her bouncers? Although, thinking about it, it was probably her brother who hired them, after all, he was at the club when we were there.'

Zak stopped and grabbed Jenny's arm. 'What did you say?'

'Oops!' Jenny giggled. 'She asked me not to say anything. But I don't suppose it matters now anyway.'

'So Mercedes' brother was at the Terra Firma last Friday?'

'Yes, but don't tell her I told you.'

'Why didn't she say anything?'

Jenny shook her head. 'He was entertaining clients, apparently. Meeting some blokes in the building trade and she didn't want you to get the wrong idea.'

'I don't get it . . .' Zak began, then stopped in his tracks. They were standing at one end of Laverne's kitchen, which was the size of a small aircraft hanger and at the other end, near the French windows into the garden, was the cause of Zak's abrupt halt. He turned round immediately, linked arms with Jenny and Donovan and steered them both back out into the hall as quickly as he could without drawing attention to himself.

'Zak!' Jenny protested. 'The party's in the opposite direction.'

'Don't look now, but the blokes we saw last week, the ones who run the Terra Firma, are here – all of them – in Mercedes' kitchen.'

'It's OK. That's what I was saying – they're probably her brother's friends,' Jenny explained innocently.

'Oh, thank gawd!' Laverne Bent teetered downstairs, leaned over the banister and interrupted their conversation. 'Jen, darlin' see if you can get the stroppy little mare to get herself into gear, will you? I don't know what the 'ell she's doing up there but she ain't opening the door to me.' Laverne had opted for a Madonna-cum-Dolly Parton image, complete with tooled leather stiletto-heeled boots and matching Stetson.

'Of course, Mrs Bent.'

Laverne cocked her head on one side and screwed up her nose in a gesture of affection. 'Aw! Ain't she polite?' she said, in the vague direction of the boys, before continuing downstairs and out towards the garden. 'Tel! 'Ave you seen where I put my pina colada? Tel! Terry? Where are you?'

Upstairs, Jenny tapped on the door of Mercedes' room while the two boys stood out of sight round the corner.

'I told you, I'll be down in a second,' Mercedes called out.

'It's me – Jenny.'

There was the sound of a key turning and then the door was thrown open. 'I thought I told you not to come!'

'No, you didn't, actually,' Jenny challenged. 'You

told me it would be crap and that it wouldn't be worth it.' Jenny walked over to the window and looked out on the scene below. 'And it doesn't look like either of those things is true.'

Mercedes couldn't help but be astounded at the level of self-confidence her friend appeared to have developed in the past week. She wasn't sure whether it was as a result of working in an all-male environment at Kwik-Fit or because she had, at long last, found a boyfriend. Either way, she decided it suited her and, in any other circumstances, she would have welcomed it. Right now though, all she wanted was the old Jenny who would do everything Mercedes said, more or less, including going home immediately.

'Jenny, it really is not a good idea for you to be here. There are things going on that you couldn't possibly imagine and I don't want you to be involved.' She went over and stood next to her friend looking out of her window at the scene below, gathering her thoughts.

The spit had been turning since breakfast and had produced a greasy haze across the garden which did little to help the humidity of the afternoon. A sizeable queue of people, lining up for slices of pork, was just discernible through the fog. There was a jazz band playing down by the tennis court and a man on stilts was juggling skittles to the pleasure of about two dozen children, none of whom Mercedes knew. In fact, there were very few people she recognised. Her nan was there of course, laughing raucously with her Great Aunt Lil who must be in her nineties. Mercedes hadn't seen Lil since her father's funeral and the old lady had been as deaf as a post and reliant on a zimmer frame then. The only difference, eight years on, was that she'd upgraded her walking frame to a wheelchair and needed to have everything addressed to her at a decibel level louder than a sonic boom.

'I said,' she heard her nan bellow, 'I 'ope they do "Bohemian Rhapsody". It's my favourite.'

'I prefer blackcurrant, myself,' she heard the old lady reply.

'Look, don't worry,' Jenny said. 'Whatever it is, I want to help you.'

Mercedes remained staring out of the window. 'Jen, you don't know the half of it. Just go, please.'

Beneath her she watched her mother appear out of the French windows and head towards the pool. Terry 'Gold Fang' Tweddle was the only person swimming and he was managing to defy the laws of nature by staying on the surface despite a medallion the size of a hub-cap dangling from his neck. Laverne leant forward to speak to him and Mercedes noticed her mother's outfit for the first time. She shook her head in despair. Why go to all the trouble of having her nails airbrushed with a tropical sunset and then wear a cowgirl outfit? It was as incongruous as turning up to a line dance in a hula skirt.

Jenny tried to reassure her again. 'It doesn't matter what's going on, Mercedes, we're here to support you.'

Mercedes heard the word 'we' and felt sick. She dropped her head in exasperation. 'Oh please, Jen, don't tell me you've brought Donovan.'

Jenny grinned, nervously. 'OK then, I won't tell you.'

Mercedes turned to her friend with a sense of urgency. 'Seriously, Jen. If you've brought Donovan then get him away from here – now.'

A voice that was all too familiar startled her. 'Too late!'

Mercedes looked up. She took a sharp intake of breath when she saw that Donovan had entered the room but, more importantly, Zak was standing with his back to the door and she heard the faint click of the key as he locked the door behind him.

'We've seen the bouncers on the door and the blokes from the club so, unless you've got any other skeletons lurking in the cupboard, I don't see the problem,' he said. 'So your brother mixes with some dodgy guys. No big deal.'

Mercedes slumped on her bed and ran her hands through her hair. Skeletons in the cupboard? She'd need a wardrobe the size of Chingford Cemetery to house all the skeletons her family were hiding. She looked up at Zak and a mini earthquake spread outwards from just below her navel. God, he was gorgeous. It was only four days since she'd seen him but he seemed to have grown more fabulous even in that short time. Well, she had nothing to lose now, she supposed. She did a quick reckoning of the odds on him still being interested in her if she told him the truth. They couldn't be that bad; after all, he was here, wasn't he? He hadn't fallen at the first fence, so she'd probably offer twenty to one. OK, there was a risk but then, isn't there with most things in life? And on this occasion, she had everything to gain and nothing to lose.

She took a deep breath. 'I want to talk to Zak,' she said to Jenny. 'Alone.' She indicated her head in the direction of the en suite bathroom. 'Will you and Donovan go in there for a while but make sure you lock the door at the other side. Chubby's room opens into it as well and the last thing you want is for him disturbing you to take a pee.'

Once Jenny and Donovan had left them, Mercedes indicated for Zak to sit on the bed next to her. She looked him in the eye, almost defying him to judge her on what she was about to tell him. Then, slowly, she told him everything.

In the en suite bathroom next door, Jenny could hardly believe her good fortune. Being shut in a room with Donovan was like the fulfilment of a lifetime's dream. Eagerly, she locked the door to Mercedes' bedroom behind her while Donovan went to the door at the other side and pulled it to. No sooner had she heard the door clicked shut than she wrapped her arms around his waist, pulled him to face her and, ignoring his gasp of surprise, she pulled him forwards by the front of his shirt and locked her lips on to his like a suction pump on to a blocked drain.

Much to her disappointment Donovan pulled away. 'Jeez, Jenny! Ease up will you? I would like to be able to use my mouth again.'

Jenny looked down, embarrassed. 'Sorry,' she said. 'I just thought we should make the most of being alone.'

Donovan raised his eyebrows cheekily. 'I'm not arguing with that,' he grinned. 'But there's making the most of it and not being able to enjoy the hog roast later on – and there's making the most of it like this.'

Tenderly, he lowered his mouth to hers so that their lips barely brushed. A quiver ran through her body and her knees began to buckle. Jenny was on the point of emitting a murmur of joyful appreciation when Donovan broke away and put his finger to his lips. There were voices in the bedroom next door; male voices and one in particular did not sound happy. Jenny saw Donovan's eyes go to the bolt on the door, which he'd been about to slide across earlier when she'd kissed him. It was still unlocked.

'Just going for a jimmy and I'll be with you in a second,' said a voice that she recognised as Mercedes' brother, Chubby.

As the door handle began to turn, Jenny felt herself stop breathing. Her eyes opened wide. She'd met Chubby a couple of times and she knew that Mercedes always spoke fondly of him, but she didn't relish the thought of being caught in his bathroom in the middle of a snogging session – especially if he was with his dodgy mates.

Swiftly, Donovan leaned over and slid the bolt across. The handle turned. When the door failed to open they watched as it was rattled hard.

'Merce? You in there?' Chubby called.

Jenny and Donovan held their breath.

'Merce! Open up, will you?'

Another voice spoke sharply. 'For gawd's sake, Chubbs, either hold it or use Mum's.'

'Yes, but she's been in there for ages, Frankie. Do you think she's all right?'

'Course she's bleedin' all right. She's sulking, that's all; that's what teenage gels do – remember?' The final remark was followed by a cruel snigger and Jenny heard footsteps leave the room. The voice that must have belonged to Mercedes' other brother Frankie, spoke again. 'Crikey, 'Orace, how the 'ell did I get 'im for a twin?' The response was an indiscernible murmur. Then, 'Gary says 'e's only gone and invited that bird.'

There was more muttering before Chubby returned.

'What's going on?' he asked.

'I was just telling 'Orace that Nick's delivered the gear to the lock-up and 'e's on 'is way over 'ere now. Tone and Kev's coming later when they've picked up the boiler suits and ski masks but I've told Sid to steer clear. I want 'is nose kept well clean.'

Donovan looked at Jenny and his eyes narrowed. He wasn't sure what he was overhearing but he didn't like the sound of it one little bit.

'And I 'ear you've invited that Myrtle bird too.'

Chubby coughed, apologetically. 'Erm, yeah.'

' 'Ell's flamin' bells with bleedin' knobs on, Chubby! Why? I do not Christmas Eve you sometimes!'

'I like her, Frankie.'

'I don't give a flying fig if you like 'er or not. I like a nice vindaloo but I ain't invited one this afternoon, 'ave I?' There was the sound of Frankie's footsteps pacing angrily. 'Jeez, Chubbs, who you gonna go out with next time – DC Polly Plod of New Scotland Yard? Are you deliberately trying to ruin the firm or what?'

The third man spoke. 'Take it easy, son. It ain't a problem. Sid ain't coming and the only others she might recognise will be from the site anyway.'

'Yeah, you're right 'Orace. But the conversation had better stay legit today. Not a dicky bird about anything to do with the blag until the meet tomorrow.' There was a pause. 'Is that crystal, Chubbs?'

' 'Course it is.' Another pause. 'Where is the meet, Frankie? Only Kev said it weren't at 'is place no more.'

'Nah – Leonie's only gone and arranged a bleedin' tupperware party, hasn't she? So, it's down the lock-up, three o'clock sharp. And, play your cards right and there might be something in it for you.'

Jenny thought it sounded as though the conversation was coming to a close, so she stretched her arms up and wrapped them around Donovan's neck in the hope of resuming where they had left off. As she did so, her hand knocked a tin of shaving foam on a glass shelf above the washbasin and it fell, hitting the porcelain bowl with a resounding clatter. Instantly the door was being banged with such force that it seemed as though it would break into a thousand splinters.

'Merce! Is that you? Open this door!'

Hurriedly, Donovan pushed Jenny in the direction of the door to Mercedes' room.

Zak had listened without speaking as Mercedes brought him up to scratch with everything she had discovered about her family. When she'd finished he took her chin and raised her face so that she was looking straight at him.

'So, you finished with me to try and protect me?' he asked in a tone of appreciation.

Mercedes nodded.

'Wow! No one's ever tried to save me from gaol before,' he teased.

Mercedes bit her bottom lip nervously. She'd taken a huge gamble and she still didn't know if it had paid off. He could walk out and ring the Old Bill right now if he chose.

'So, how were you planning to pull off this single-handed Miss Marple act?'

Mercedes shrugged. 'I'm working on it.'

He nodded as though giving her answer some thought, 'Do you fancy a partner in anti-crime, to work on it with you?' he asked, slowly moving so close that their lips almost touched.

The next instant they heard the key turn in the lock. The door to the en suite bathroom burst open and Jenny and Donovan tumbled into the bedroom with eyes like Bart Simpson's. From the other end of the bathroom Mercedes could hear Frankie shouting and banging. She walked through the bathroom, unbolted the door into Chubby's room and threw it open.

Staring her brother in the eye, she stood, legs akimbo and arms folded. 'What!'

Frankie peered over her shoulder and, seeing Zak on her bed, his jaw set. 'What's 'e doing 'ere?'

'Minding his own business.'

'Don't get mouthy with me, Merce,' he warned.

Mercedes opened her arms in a gesture of feigned

innocence. 'Simply answering your question, Frankie.'

Frankie's eyes darted from Mercedes to Zak, suspiciously. ' 'Ave you been locked in the bathroom with 'im?'

Mercedes folded her arms again. 'No, actually, I've been locked in my bedroom with him.' She derived a tingle of satisfaction when she saw Frankie twitch with annoyance. 'Talking,' she added with some glee.

'So why d'you need to lock the door? What're you hiding?'

'*I'm* not hiding anything,' she said, pointedly. 'I simply wanted some privacy.' Frankie seemed unconvinced but she was not to be intimidated. 'Now, if you don't mind, Frankie, I haven't finished my conversation yet. If you need a pee, use Mum's bathroom, or the guest bathroom or the downstairs cloakroom. Oh, and by the way, you know I'm babysitting for you tomorrow night when Cheryl goes to see the Muscle Men? Well, Zak will be coming too.' Frankie opened his mouth to protest. 'So that'll save you some money on cab fares. But, on the down side, I've put my rates up.'

She closed the door in his face, slid the bolt across and returned to her friends.

'Man, you were phenomenal!' Donovan said.

'Thank you,' she smiled. 'Amazing what a little bit of information that he wouldn't like his wife to find out, can do to increase your courage. Now, tell me what you heard.'

When Jenny had finished relating the glorious technicolor account of the men's conversation, Donovan gave her the straight version.

Mercedes smiled. At last, she had the beginnings of a plan.

'OK, what are we waiting for?' She stood up and took Zak's hand. 'Let's go party!'

Eleven

The storm that had been threatening for the past week broke just as Mercedes put the key into the padlock that secured the small door at one side of the metal roll-up entrance to her brother's lock-up. Stealing the key from Chubby's key ring had been remarkably easy; it had the letters LU written on it in red paint, just as his house keys had H1 and H2 on them and his office key had O on it. Much as Mercedes loved her brother, she often wondered if he'd been taking a nap when common sense was being given out.

The lock-up was in the middle of a row of railway arches just off Leyton High Road and, on the wet Sunday afternoon, there was no one else around. Cautiously, she stepped over the metal strip at the foot of the door and into the dank interior. She slipped off her trainers to avoid leaving wet footprints on the concrete floor and took a deep steadying breath. A train rumbled overhead just as a clap of thunder split the sultry Sunday afternoon, echoing through the empty space and causing her to start.

'I want to stay with you,' said Zak.

'No!' Mercedes was adamant. 'We've been over this a dozen times. I want you to lock me in and then go away – right out of the area. I don't want you or your car anywhere near here at three o'clock when they arrive.'

'I'm not happy about this.'

She pulled his head through the doorway towards her and kissed him on the lips. 'I know you're not. Now lock the door and go. I'll put my mobile on silent and I'll text you to pick me up when it's all over.' Zak was about to protest but she leaned forwards and kissed him again. 'Just go!' And she pulled the door to.

Once she'd heard the door being locked, Mercedes took some time for her eyes to adjust to the dark, then took a small torch out of her pocket and flashed it round the interior; it hadn't changed a bit! Despite the humidity outside, inside the lock-up it was as cold as a mortuary. The sound of the rain and a slow dripping of water coming from somewhere to her left did little to make it feel more homely. Mercedes stood for a moment reflecting on the last time she'd been there. It had been a regular treat when she was small, to come here with her dad. She would sit on his leather swivel chair while he attended to business.

It was almost as though she could hear him now. 'You'd better keep your sunny shut, mate, or I'll tuck you up good and proper and make sure you go away for a long stretch.'

Another train went over, rattling the fabric of the building and startling her back to the present. She gave a shudder, this was no time for sentimentality. Part of her was tempted to agree to Zak's offer to stay but she knew it was too risky. If *she* got caught at least she'd got her family ties to fall back on; that and the little matter of Frankie's relationship with Honey Coombes. She wasn't quite sure what her story was going to be but she was hoping that, as it was half an hour before the meet, she'd have time to look around and find some inspiration.

She shone the torch up to the vaulted ceiling and then along the depth of the cavernous workshop right to the back. In the centre of the building were two shapes that were obviously cars, covered with tarpaulins. At the back, another tarpaulin covered a pile of something that she couldn't make out and there was also a long row of trestle tables near the back wall as well as what had been her father's office at the far end, separated from the main area by glass partitions.

Ignoring the cars she slowly made her way to the back. The door to the office was open. With some trepidation she went in and sat in the large leather swivel chair again – just for old time's sake. She shone her torch over the papers on the desk, looking for something – but she didn't know what. There were some letters she didn't understand from an address in the Cayman islands. They were addressed to a 'James Squires' and seemed to be related to the purchase of the casino next to the bank. But what were they doing in her brothers' lock-up?

She flashed the torch over the desk and noticed something else interesting – and this she *did* understand. It was a copy of *Chic-Chick* magazine. Although Mercedes initially thought it a little odd that either of her siblings should be interested in women's fashion, the reason for the magazine's presence became glaringly obvious when she saw the cover. There, pouting seductively from the glossy jacket, was Honey Coombes. Mercedes checked her watch; it was two thirty five. She still had some time so, taking care not to disturb the other papers on the desk, she opened the magazine. On page four, under the heading, 'Chic-Chick Chat' there were more photographs of the model, this time on the arm of some other man. Mercedes ran her torch over the photograph and shivered at his cold dark eyes. She moved closer so that she could read the caption:

The words *bees* and *pot* certainly applied to supermodel Honey Coombes when she attended the premier of Jay Ridley's latest film, *Grab*, last week. And the buzzword was that one of those swarming for her attention was none other than millionaire playboy Jonathon Sabatini pictured here.

The note she had read in Frankie's study had mentioned a Jonnie 'Schizo' Sabatini and she thought the odds on there being two Sabatinis with first names of the Jonnie/Jonathon genre were so remote they didn't even warrant doing the maths. And hadn't the note said that he was going to do over her brothers, in the pay of Spinks? Mercedes felt sick. She didn't want her family involved in the robbery in the first place but she certainly didn't want them to then get done over by their arch-rival's firm, especially if he was employing someone affectionately known as 'Schizo'. What she couldn't work out was why her brothers seemed to be going ahead with it even though they knew. And who had told them? She had a sudden recollection of the slinky cow of a woman at the club tucking a note into Frankie's top pocket shortly before she kissed him. Was that the same note that Mercedes had seen? In which case did that mean that Honey Coombes was on Frankie's side or the schizo guy's?

The throaty sound of a car being revved outside alerted her and Mercedes realised that she had wasted precious minutes that she'd intended using to find a hiding place. She closed the magazine and shone the torch around the cramped office. There was nowhere there to conceal herself for any length of time. She went back out into the main area and flashed the torch over the space. She could hear both her brothers' voices now and the heavy sound of metal banging on metal as they opened the padlock. She was frantic. The only place that she could conceal herself was under the tarpaulin right at the back so she switched off her torch and slid between a pile of old car tyres and the wall before dragging the heavy fabric over her hair just as the fluorescent lights flickered on.

'You are something else, you know that, Chubbs? How can you 'ave lost it?'

'I dunno. I could've sworn I put it on my keyring when Nick gave it back to me.'

Mercedes felt a twinge of guilt that she was the cause of Chubby getting it in the neck from Frankie again, and made a mental promise to make it right with him when all this was over. Then she snuggled down behind the dirty tyres and prepared for the long haul.

At three o'clock sharp, just as Frankie had ordained, it started.

'Where's Sid?' he asked, drumming his fingers on the top of the table.

'Said 'e might be a bit late,' Gary replied.

There was a communal sharp intake of breath. It was obvious to all those gathered around the tables that being late for one of Frankie's meetings was not a good idea for anyone who had even the slightest interest in self-preservation.

'Right then, for those of us who can be bothered to be here on time, let's see what we've got,' Frankie continued. 'Let's start with you, Nick. What little delights did you manage to locate for us?'

The small Greek dragged a bundle of bin bags from under the table and placed them carefully on the top. He pulled out what looked like three rolls of blanket and proceeded to unroll them one at a time, then lay out the contents along the length of the table.

'What are these?' Frankie said, picking up one of the semi-automatic guns.

There was a slight pause. 'They're the shooters, Frankie.'

'I can see that they're the shooters, Nick.' The other men in the room shuffled uncomfortably. 'Let me put this another way. Do you remember that conversation we had in the Terra Firma?'

'Yes, Frankie. You said you wanted me to get some shooters and I asked you if you'd got any particular shooters in mind and you said, "Sort of." But then you didn't say no more so I used my initiative.'

'Really? Well, a word in your shell-like. Put your initiative back under the stone where it belongs and get them ears of yours cleaned out because I didn't say, "sort of", I said, "sawn offs". We are robbing a bank, not mobilising a coup in some former Soviet republic.' Frankie paced round the table running his hands through his hair then he picked up the third gun and tossed it along the table with disdain. 'And what is this?'

'My source could only lay his hands on two of the AK47s, so I brought my lad's air gun as well.'

'Jeez!' Frankie slapped his forehead with the heel of his hand. 'So two of us is going in with enough hardware to take out a platoon of guerrillas while the other can occupy his time popping sparrows with an air pistol?'

'Ah, well, that's the other thing, Frankie. They wouldn't be able to take out anyone 'cos my supplier had a bit of a problem with the ammo.'

'I thought you said we wasn't going to use guns, Frankie,' Chubby interrupted.

'We ain't gonna *use* them, bruv, but we want to look the part; put the frighteners on a bit if there's any aggro. Orright?'

Nick saw an opportunity and seized it. 'You see Frankie, I'm with Chubby on this 'cos I thought, if they was just for frighteners it didn't matter what they was or if they worked,' he explained with some trepidation.

Frankie waited for another train to pass before speaking. 'You see that's where you went wrong, my old Bubble and Squeak – you thought. Do not think – OK?' He took a roll of twenty pound notes from his back pocket, peeled off a hundred and handed them to Nick.

'Er, that's a bit short, isn't it, Frankie?'

'Yes, mate. But so are you and so is the order I placed, so clear off.'

As the disgruntled Greek reached the door at the other end of the lock-up, Sid entered. The atmosphere round the table was electric as the group waited for Sid to join them.

'Sorry I'm late,' he mumbled.

'You will be,' Frankie threatened. 'Now, let's check on the rest of the equipment. Kev, where's the boiler suits and masks?'

Kev heaved a sports bag on to the table and took out six ski masks and four navy blue boiler suits. He proudly spread one out along the table.

'I thought I might as well get top of the range.'

As soon as Frankie saw the boiler suit he gave Kev a look of disdain. 'There we go with that *thinking* malarkey again! How many times do I have to tell you lot that it is very dangerous to do a job when you do not have the proper equipment. And you, Kev my old china, definitely do not have whatever's necessary for thinking purposes.' He picked up the sleeve of the boiler suit and pretended to scrutinise it. 'Did you check these before you nicked them?'

'No need, Frankie. Like I said, top of the range.'

'Tone,' Frankie turned to one of the other men. 'Help me out here, mate. Where do we get the overalls for the lads down the car yard?'

'Begum's down Whitechapel,' Tone replied.

Frankie turned to Kev. 'And where did you half inch this little lot from?'

'Begum's down Whitechapel, Frankie.'

Frankie flipped over the boiler suit so that the back

of it was upwards and the words 'Bent Ent.' could be seen embroidered between the shoulders. 'You stupid plonker!' he shouted. 'What did you do for the ski masks, Kev, get your Auntie Dolly to knit 'em with everyone's names across the forehead just so the Old Bill don't have too much trouble identifying us?'

'Sorry, Frankie.'

'What is the first rule of our profession, Kev?'

'Don't nick what's already yours, Frank.'

'Sort it – tomorrow! OK?'

Kev gathered up the boiler suits and pushed them all back into the holdall.

'Chubby, you was getting the spray paint for taking out the CCTV cameras,' Frankie said, wearily.

Chubby removed two cans of car paint from his pockets and put them on the table.

Frankie lowered his head into his hands and walked round the lock-up in exasperation. When he came back to the table he sighed, heavily. 'Where d'you get these, bruv?'

'Halfords. I got a receipt.'

Frankie gripped the edge of the table and leaned forwards so that he was staring at the floor. 'Did I, or did I not, specify matt black?'

'Erm,' Chubby scratched his head.

'Not glossy black; not satin black; certainly not . . .' he picked up one of the cans and read the label, '. . . metallic jade – with sparkly bits in it!' He banged the tin down and looked at his brother. 'I said, matt black, Chubbs and that was not just because I thought it would go with the décor. It's because it obscures everything and dries the fastest.'

'Sorry, Frankie.'

Frankie straightened up and lit a cigarette. 'Dare I ask how we're doing with the walkie-talkies? Have we got the pukka goods or did we go for the Fisher Price end of the market on them an' all?'

'Sorted,' Horace reassured him, placing three handsets on the table. 'One for each driver and one for you. They're all tuned in and charged up.'

'Cheers, 'Orace. And the motors?' Frankie was visibly relieved that at least one member of the firm seemed to be on the ball.

Horace walked over to the first tarpaulin and pulled it back to reveal a silver BMW. 'Three series. Poky little job. Get us out of the square in no time.' He was a man of few words. 'Nicked in Manchester last week. False plates. Ready to go.' He went to the other car and pulled back its covering to reveal a dark blue Escort. 'Kev's car. Not as fast but not as conspicuous neither.'

'Right!' Frankie pulled out the architects' drawings of the bank and the casino and spread them on the table. 'Let's run through this one more time. Sid, talk us through it.'

The older man stepped forward and plumped up his chest. 'As you know, I will be on duty next Friday night from ten till six. There's always two of us and one of us does a check of the whole building once an hour on the hour. It takes about fifteen minutes. On Friday, at five to midnight I will suggest to my colleague that he should do the round. That way, he'll be out of the way until about ten past.'

Frankie came in. 'At this point, 'Orace will be dropping us off outside the casino before going round the block and parking in Pall Mall.'

'What about security cameras?' Tone asked.

Gary, who until then had remained silent, spoke up. 'The ones on the bank are angled on the front door and don't take in much else and,' he grinned, 'the ones on the casino ain't operational yet. Shame, innit?'

'Wouldn't it just be safer to go in at the back though?' Tone persisted.

'It would, Tone, it would,' Frankie said. 'Except that there ain't no service entrance at the back so it's the front or the front. Take your choice. But we make

193

it look like a break in. We don't want no one getting a whiff that it's an inside job.'

'Alarm?' Tone asked again.

Gary shook his head in mock regret. 'Sadly, it'll have been playing up all week and the electrician won't be able to fix it.'

There was a unanimous chuckle of approval.

Sid coughed officiously. 'So at exactly midnight Frankie and Tone are going to come through the party wall into the basement. I will look shocked and try to put up some sort of struggle but Frankie'll threaten me with a gun. Meanwhile Tone will be spraying the surveillance cameras.'

'With *matt black*,' Frankie said glaring at Chubby.

'Then,' Sid carried on, seemingly annoyed at the repeated interruptions, 'I will instruct Frankie on the combination of the safe.'

'How will you do that, Sid?' Kev asked. 'Banks don't have a habit of telling their staff the combination.'

Sid's face set. 'I ain't always been a security guard you know, Kev. I was a master locksmith for nearly thirty years – till the bloke I worked for went bankrupt.' His face contorted with resentment. 'More than a quarter of a flamin' century I'd worked for 'im and I didn't get a penny in redundancy! It weren't fair.'

'I still don't get it,' Kev said, puzzled. 'How does being a locksmith mean 'e knows the combination?'

Another clap of thunder seemed to increase Frankie's irritation. 'You don't need to get it, Kev. Sid is an expert and one of the advantages of his misspent adulthood was that he learned how to read a combination from the other side of a room. That is all you need to know.'

Kev eyed Sid suspiciously. 'Why don't we just blow it? Seems easier to me.'

'Anti-explosive device,' said Sid smugly.

Kev held Sid's glare. 'What's wrong with cutting our way in then? We done it before.'

Frankie tapped his foot impatiently. He turned to Kev. 'That was a tin-pot little number in a jeweller's. Even that took about twenty minutes. Now, end of! You was saying, Sid?'

'They change the combination every Monday,' Sid went on, 'but by Friday, I'll have had enough time to work out what they're using and it's a standard three wheel combination so that's a piece of cake.' He looked round the group. 'But both locks must be done simultaneously.'

'Cheers.' Frankie took over again. 'The money will be in bundles of notes and bonds, so me, Sid and

Tone will stash it into nylon holdalls and take them back up through the casino.'

'What about the deposit boxes?' Kev piped up again.

'Ain't time. We'd need plastic explosives and there'll be enough cash and bonds to do us all nicely this time.'

'So you're just leaving them?'

'Who's running this blag, Kev? You or me?' Frankie challenged.

Kev held up his hands in a gesture of capitulation. 'Your call, Frankie.'

'As I was saying, Sid reckons there'll be going on for five mill in there on a Friday night.' The others whistled in unison. Frankie turned to Sid. 'Then Tone'll tie you up and give you a bit of a make over, just so you look the part, and we'll be out of the building before laughing boy comes downstairs from doing his rounds. I want us in an' out in under five minutes.' Everyone nodded. ' 'Orace, I want you outside that building at dead on five past.' Frankie traced their getaway route with his finger. 'We go this way round the square and up Duke of York Street to Jermyn Street where Kev will be waiting.'

'But Frankie, it's a one-way system round there,' Chubby pointed out, 'And that would be the wrong way.'

Frankie lit another cigarette and inhaled deeply. 'Chubbs,' he said, patiently. 'We will be three geezers in boiler suits and ski masks carrying Kalashnikovs and a boot full of five million knicker. What part of that scenario suggests to you that I'm worried about going the wrong way round a one-way system?'

Chubby shrugged apologetically.

'By the time we get to Kev I want the boiler suits off. Keep the gloves and ski masks and we'll burn them when we get back here. Kev, you and 'Orace go up there this week and find a parking spot. There's a couple of places what's got cameras so steer well clear of them. Once we've transferred the gear, Kev and 'Orace will head west before turning down towards the embankment and then back here. Me and Tone will split up and get cabs or night buses and we meet back here Saturday morning at eleven o'clock. Any questions?' No one said anything. 'Right then, we'll meet here on Friday at half ten. Be lucky!'

When the group had dispersed, Mercedes wriggled to try and regain some feeling in her legs and bum. She heard the door shut at the other end of the lock-up but the lights were still on and she could hear muffled voices. She checked her watch. It was five thirty. Just enough time to call Zak to pick her up, go home, get changed, have something to eat and be at Frankie's to babysit at eight o'clock. Perfect. She rolled her neck and stretched her arms as she thought of all the things she needed to put into action now that she knew exactly how the robbery was going to take place. All she needed was the last of the gang to go home so that she could get on with her plan. She began to push her feet into her trainers ready to leave, when Frankie's voice sounded from just the other side of the tyres.

'There's something I didn't mention to the lads,' she heard him say, although she wasn't sure to whom. 'We've got a grass.'

There was a murmur of unrest. Frankie lowered his voice so that she could only just make out what he was saying.

'Someone's stitched us up with Spinks and 'e intends to do us over once we've done the dirty work. We been had – hook, line and flamin' sinker.'

The gruff voice of Uncle Horace sounded. 'Any ideas?'

'Well, my money's on Kev. He's a cocky little pilchard with an eye for the main chance so that's why I'm going to leave him out of it.'

'You're not still going ahead, are you?' Chubby asked.

'Course! Gone too far down the line to call it off now, so that means you're back in as number two driver, Chubbs – only I want you parked in King Street. We'll need another motor though.'

'Cheers, bruv. What sort?' Chubby sounded enthusiastic.

Frankie hesitated. ' 'Orace will sort that. All right, 'Orace?'

'No problems. I fancy a day in Brighton tomorrow.'

'Good.'

Mercedes wished they would just clear off and let her get out of there. Why couldn't they have this discussion at home? Frankie threw down his cigarette end and Mercedes watched in alarm as the glowing butt rolled towards where she was concealed. It rocked to a halt next to a puddle of oil that was only inches from the edge of the tarpaulin. If that went up, she stood as much chance of getting out of there as yesterday's hog roast did of foraging in a field again. Her eyes widened in terror. If only she could stretch her foot out and step on it – but it was too risky. Another train went overhead and between the clunking of the metal wheels she could just make out the sound of footsteps diminishing. Quickly, she reached forwards and stubbed out the smouldering remains of her brother's bad habit.

When this was all over, that was something else she was going to speak to him about.

'Cheers then,' she heard Frankie say from the other end of the lock-up. The door was obviously open because she could hear the rain pelting on to the road outside. She heard muffled voices then Frankie responded. 'Nah! I've got paperwork to do here. I'll see you down the club later.' The metal door swung shut.

That was all she needed: just as she'd been hoping to make her escape, Frankie had decided to stay. From her position behind the tyres she watched him go into the office. He picked up the phone then sat on one corner of the desk.

'All right, darling?' she heard him ask. She'd give fifty to one it wasn't Cheryl on the other end.

After what seemed like an eternity, Mercedes checked her watch; he'd been on the phone for almost an hour. It was already half past six and she needed to get out of there. Frankie changed his position on the desk so that his back was to the main area and she decided to take her chance. Shuffling backwards along the tunnel of tyres she made her way to the far side of the lock-up. There was a tight gap between the tyres and the wall but she reckoned she could just about get through. Then, if she was careful, she could make a dash for the cover of the cars. After that it wasn't far to the door, provided she didn't make a noise and attract his attention. She sent Zak a text to tell him to be outside in ten minutes.

Already here came the reply. **R U OK?**

Frankie on phone. Can't get out.

Don't do anything. Wait there he instructed.

Mercedes crouched down behind the BMW and folded her arms. Now what was he going to do? Much as she liked Zak, she wished he'd stick to the investment side of banking and leave this to her.

Zak's shirt stuck to his skin as the rain continued to lash the streets of Leyton. He'd been parked in a side street all afternoon and had witnessed the majority of the men leaving. Now he was standing outside the lock-up, getting worried. He needed to get Mercedes home for her babysitting appointment, and the last person he'd wanted to be between him and his goal was her psycho-nutter brother. Somehow, he had to draw him out of there. And the means of doing that was right next to him; Frankie's black Carrera 911. He remembered an occasion some years ago; his normally passive father had erupted with rage when a lorry scraped the side of his brand new car. His mother had shaken her head and sighed, 'The way to a man's anger is through his pride.' So, that was what Zak was going to do; prey on Frankie's weakness and threaten his pride and joy. He sent Mercedes another text:

As soon as F leaves run 2 Lea Brdg Rd. Mt me @ Baker's Arms in 5 mins.

Zak didn't want to damage the vehicle, he had too much admiration for the car to do that, but he wanted Frankie to *think* he was damaging it. So, gathering up an assortment of plastic bottles and crisp packets from the bin outside a nearby newsagent's, he placed them in a mound on the bonnet of the Porsche. When everything was in place, he put his foot against the wheel and gave it a hefty kick, setting off the alarm. Within seconds Frankie appeared at the door of the lock-up and the alarm bleeped off. Zak, standing far enough away to be seen but not identified, ran off conspicuously.

'Come 'ere you little toe-rag!' Frankie shouted, heading after him in the opposite direction from Lea Bridge Road.

Zak knew there'd been a reason why he'd been in the school athletic squad. He ran for all he was worth then turned into one of the residential side streets that was lined with terrace houses. The storm had darkened the July evening prematurely and most houses had their lights on. Choosing one that was in darkness, Zak vaulted the hedge and crouched down in the front garden until Frankie, realising that he'd lost sight of this quarry, swore loudly before kicking over a dustbin in disgust and heading back toward the lock-up. Zak gave an almost imperceptible punch of satisfaction; His plan had worked – well, at least *his* part of it had. He only hoped Mercedes had got out when she'd had the chance.

Five minutes later he pulled up outside the Baker's Arms, leaned across and opened the passenger door. God, she was beautiful! Mercedes slipped into the car and, tossing her wet hair out of her face, she smiled at him.

Zak pushed the car into gear and returned her smile. 'So, are we a team? Or are we a team?'

She looked across at him and appeared to give the question some thought. 'OK,' she agreed. 'On one condition though – for the rest of this game, I'm the captain.' She checked her watch. 'And, we'd better get a move on because we're playing again in just over an hour.'

'Are you serious?'

'Absolutely.' Mercedes smiled. 'Don't worry though; this time won't be as dangerous.'

Zak eyed her dubiously.

'We're going to break into my brother's study so, as his neighbour, you'll be practically playing on home turf!'

Twelve

Jenny could hardly contain her excitement. She'd been all set for a boring Sunday evening sitting in front of a documentary on the meerkats of the Kalahari with her father tutting over the state of the world from behind his Sunday papers on one side while her mother clicked over her knitting needles at the other, when her mobile had flashed up with a message.

Zak pickin U up @ 8. Goin to F's to suss out wots happnin. C U there. M xx

She'd lost no time in texting Donovan. Fancy babysitn 2nite? B ready @ 8.05.

As eight o'clock approached, Jenny gave little thought to the original message from Mercedes but was focusing all her anticipation on the one she'd sent Donovan. This would be the second time in two days that she'd seen him and she was hopping up and down by the window like a hedgehog on hot tarmac.

'When are we going to meet this young man, Jennifer?' her mother said from behind a pattern for an Arran cardigan.

'Erm,' Jenny hesitated, as the word 'never' struggled to be voiced. 'Oh, he's very shy,' she said, crossing her fingers behind her back.

There was the honk of a car horn and Jenny ran out of the house and down the path before her mother could finish her stitch. But, any plans she'd been making for a cosy evening as a foursome were dashed when she saw En Min sitting in the passenger seat.

'Oh – hi, En,' she said through a forced smile. 'What're you doing here?'

En Min shrugged. 'Your guess is as good as mine. I just got a weird call from Mercedes telling me she needed my help.'

Jenny was put out. Mercedes hadn't said anything about needing *her* help.

'So did I,' she said. 'Exciting, isn't it?' Then before En Min could reply, she turned to Zak. 'I said we'd pick Donovan up on the way. Is that OK?'

Zak hesitated. 'Fine by me – does Mercedes know?'

'She's cool,' Jenny hedged, crossing her fingers once again.

However, when they arrived at the house in St Drogo's Avenue, it was apparent to everyone that Mercedes was anything but cool about Donovan's presence.

The second they stepped over the threshold, Jenny found herself being dragged the length of the galleried hall and into Cheryl's kitchen.

Mercedes folded her arms and addressed her in a harsh whisper. 'Why the hell have you brought him, Jen?'

Jenny was put out. 'Well, Zak's here, isn't he?' she offered by way of explanation.

Mercedes frowned as though she was trying to follow the logic behind Jenny's statement. 'So? This isn't a date, you know? We're here to do a job tonight, Jen. You're my lookout in case the kids wake up or Frankie comes home early. I need you to be focused.'

'I will be focused,' Jenny said, gazing over Mercedes' shoulder and giving a little wave to Donovan who was in the hall with the others.

'I can't afford for you two to go off for a snogging session on the settee while we're in the study. You have to stay alert.'

Jenny gave a sigh of irritation. She didn't know what had got into Mercedes recently. She'd never really been one for the dramatic but she was beefing this up like some West End production. 'Er, hello! This is your brother, you know, not the Wanstead Mafia.'

Mercedes rubbed her forehead in frustration. 'This is serious, Jen. Frankie might not be in the Mafia but this is hardly Little League, either.' Jenny raised her eyes skyward as though doubting the statement. 'You know we heard those guys in the caff talking about Nick the Bubble?'

Jenny nodded.

'Well he's an arms dealer!'

Jenny peered into the hall and smiled at Donovan. 'What sort of arms dealer?' she asked, distractedly.

Mercedes slapped the heel of her hand against her forehead, exasperated. 'What do you mean, what *sort of* arms dealer? How many sorts are there? We're not talking prosthetic limbs, you know!'

Jenny drew her attention back to her friend and stared at her blankly. Then, as the full realisation of what had been said registered, her eyes widened in horror. 'Oh my god! You don't mean guns?'

Mercedes sighed. 'No, Jen; they're going to rush into the bank with false fingers blazing. Of course I mean guns!'

Jenny felt the colour drain from her face. 'I don't believe this! This is awful! This is terrible!' She looked at her friend mutinously. 'How could you get me involved in this?'

Mercedes tried to reassure her. 'It'll be OK as long as we keep our heads.'

'Yeah, well – with guns flying around, that's

going to be easier said than done,' Jenny replied, sarcastically. 'Do the others know?'

'Only Zak.'

The knowledge that she had been chosen to be privy to the information above En Min went a small way towards mollifying her – but only a small way. Jenny was annoyed and scared and there was only one sensible thing to do – they had to get out. They should go home and forget the conversations they'd overheard. They should just pretend that none of it had ever happened and that everything was back to normal.

Mercedes tried to placate her. 'It's not as bad as it sounds – they've got guns but no bullets apparently.'

'Oh, well that makes all the difference!' This was not what Jenny had had in mind when she'd invited Donovan to babysit with her tonight. She cast another glance out into the hall – he was so gorgeous and it might be a whole week before she had the chance to see him again. Perhaps it wasn't too late to talk sense into Mercedes and salvage something of the evening, after all.

'Look,' she suggested, 'I've had a brilliant idea, why don't we just call the whole thing off and spend a nice evening together? The five of us – and maybe Zak can get someone round here for En Min?' she said lightly, as though raising her voice half an octave would make the idea more appealing. 'Then we'll just go home and they can get on with their robbery. Or,' she beamed as a thought struck her, 'maybe that wasn't even what they were talking about . . . maybe we've just imagined . . .'

Mercedes sighed. 'If you want to go home, Jen, you can do, but it's too late for me. There's no going back.'

Their conversation was interrupted by Zak. 'Everything OK here?'

'No,' Jenny said, in a voice that sounded more like her parents' budgie than her own.

'Yes, I'm just coming,' Mercedes replied.

Zak walked over to the sink and picked up the opened bottle of red wine that was on the worktop. Jenny couldn't believe he was so calm when he knew about the guns. And now, it seemed, he was about to start helping himself to a master criminal's alcohol supply! Had he and Mercedes suddenly developed a death wish? Maybe they'd agreed on one of those suicide pacts and they'd decided to drag Jenny along for the ride.

'Zak!' she warned. 'Put it down.'

'Interesting,' he said, holding out the bottle towards the girls as though he were a wine waiter. 'Would Mademoiselle care to sample Château No-label. A very good vintage I'm told.' He chuckled and spoke to Mercedes. 'So your brother doesn't limit his robberies to banks then?'

Mercedes shook her head and frowned. 'What do you mean?'

Zak put down the bottle and took another from the wine rack. 'Look,' he said.

'I'm looking.' Mercedes was obviously perplexed.

Zak took down another and held it out to her. 'Doesn't it strike you as a bit odd?'

Jenny was as puzzled as her friend. So, Mercedes' brother and his wife liked to drink wine; didn't most people these days? She knew her own parents referred to it as 'the devil's liquor' but then, her parents were so old fashioned they thought Windows 2000 was a double glazing catalogue.

'What are you on about?' Mercedes said.

Zak replaced the bottles in the rack and then planted a kiss on Mercedes' head. 'It means they're dodgy: nicked, half inched, illicit, contraband – whatever you want to call it,' he explained gently. 'Why else would they have had their labels soaked off?'

Jenny was astounded. Mercedes looked none too pleased either. Her face set.

She turned to Jenny. 'You see, Jen; this is why it

has to stop. For as long as I can remember my family have been drinking wines and spirits without labels and I'd never even questioned it before.'

Jenny suddenly felt overwhelming sympathy for her friend. What else in Mercedes' life was of dubious origin, she wondered? The clothes she herself had so often been lent? The beautiful home that she coveted; their cars; even Mercedes' school fees – were they all the results of her family's sticky-fingered lifestyle? Was there anything about her, (other than her friends, of course) that wasn't tainted?

'Hey, you don't suppose that Tiffany necklace that your brother gave y—' she began.

'Don't even go there, Jen,' Mercedes sighed. 'I've already decided the odds of it being stolen are at least eleven to four. So, are you in or are you out?'

Jenny went across and put her arms round her friend and hugged her. 'I'm in.'

'Right!' Mercedes said. 'We've wasted enough time. Come on.'

She positioned Jenny and Donovan at the foot of the stairs from where they could see both the front door and the study on the ground floor yet were also within sight of the children's rooms on the landing. The slightest sign of movement and Mercedes wanted them primed to alert the others.

Donovan put his arm round Jenny's shoulder and shrugged. 'I'd always thought of myself as a bit of an Action Man but I suppose lookout is cool.'

'Oh, lookout is *very* cool,' Jenny agreed, snuggling up to him.

'Jen? Focus!' Mercedes sighed. 'The back door's unlocked – just in case Frankie or Cheryl come home early and any of us need to make a hasty exit. Now, let's get on.'

Mercedes took a deep breath and approached the door to Frankie's study. She tapped in the security code then, carefully, she turned the knob and pushed. Nothing. Perhaps she'd pressed a wrong number? She steadied herself and tried again. It was no good; the door would not open. She hung her head in anger and frustration – this could not be happening!

'You know what's happened?' she said to Zak. 'He's only gone and taken a leaf out of Boreham's book and changed the blooming code! I can't believe it!'

Zak put a comforting arm around her. 'Let's think about this logically. Anyone who uses his date of birth is hardly the brightest crayon in the pack, so he's probably just chosen someone else's. How about his kids'?' he suggested.

'Brilliant!'

She tapped in Alfie's date of birth, first forwards and then backwards. Nothing. Then she tried Paige's but the door remained firmly shut.

'What about your other brother's?' Jenny piped up.

Mercedes looked at Jenny and took a deep breath. She couldn't help feeling that it might have been better for everyone if she'd let Jenny go when she'd first started to bottle it. 'They're twins, Jenny – think about it.'

Jenny grimaced apologetically. 'Oops.'

When Mercedes had exhausted every member of the extended Bent family, alive and dead, she sank to the floor and dropped her head into her hands. She had to get into that room and find the file. She couldn't believe that after all this effort she was going to have to abandon her plans and just sit back and watch her brothers pursue their life of crime.

'What about the woman he was with at the club,' Zak suggested, '– Honey Coombes?'

Mercedes sprang to her feet and kissed him. 'You are a genius.'

He grinned. 'So it's been rumoured.'

Zak was dispatched to his home, two doors away, to look up the supermodel's date of birth on the Internet and, five minutes later, Mercedes, Zak and

En Min were inside Frankie's office while Jenny and Donovan kept watch outside.

The folder had been tossed back on to his desk but the contents were just as she remembered.

'Here,' Mercedes said, handing all the handwritten notes to En Min. 'I want you to copy all these as precisely as you can. Do you think you can do that?'

'No problems. This is like Reception Class stuff compared to getting Fern's homework past the old Doberman.'

'Now,' she said, leading Zak to Frankie's computer. 'Before I can close down my brother's illegal activities, I need to know exactly what's going on in his life legally, so let's see what joys this will reveal.'

Mercedes reasoned, correctly as it turned out, that with Frankie's limited creative streak, working out his password would be a doddle. As far as she could see, there were only three things in life that Frankie cared about; his children, his mistress and his car – not necessarily in that order.

'A piece of cake,' she grinned as Zak typed Carrera 911 and the computer sprang into life.

She directed him to Frankie's Internet banking account but Zak was pessimistic.

'It's not going to work,' he warned. 'Even if we guess all the passwords and personal information, there's no way we'll work out his PIN number.'

Mercedes smiled. 'Oh ye of little faith. Four, eight, two, seven.' She tucked her thumbs into her belt and stretched her chin forward in a chicken-like way, a habit Frankie had developed believing it made him appear more assertive. She dropped her voice and spoke in a heavy East End accent. 'You see, Chubbs, what you gotta do is pick a number what you can remember. Me, for instance, I use house numbers – this one and your one in Honey Drive. Forty eight, twenty seven – lemon squeezy, mate.' She dropped the impression and kissed Zak lightly. 'You forget I come from a long line of criminal master-idiots.'

When they were all done, Mercedes picked up the plans of the bank. 'The only thing that's a bit tricky now is how to get these architects' drawings copied. En, this is your field – any ideas?'

En Min shrugged. 'We've got a print machine at work for copying drawings that size, but if I took them now, wouldn't your brother realise they were missing?'

'Probably.' Then she smiled as a solution to her problem presented itself. 'But Mum's got a spare set of keys for here at home and on Monday afternoons Cheryl takes Paige to a toddler club and Frankie'll be at the car yard.' She grinned at Zak. 'I'll just have to pull a sickie at work.'

The first part of Operation Stitch-up was completed in less than an hour and the house returned to normal. Mercedes stood on Frankie's doorstep with her arms round Zak.

'I'll probably see you in the morning,' she said quietly. 'I'll say I've got a dental appointment and need to leave at lunchtime.'

'Why don't you take the whole day, it would make more sense.'

She shook her head. 'I've got a few things I need to sort out with my old friend Harley 'Tosis Spinks on the train in the morning.'

He kissed her softly. 'You know that I'm with you a hundred percent on this but just be careful, won't you?'

Mercedes rested her head on his chest, relieved and grateful. No one had been with her a hundred percent since her dad died.

'Swede 'art, swede 'art, get back in the car, darlin'.' Harry Spinks, although not averse to the physical discomfort of anyone else, was beside himself at seeing his daughter's agony.

Harley Spinks eased herself, painfully, from one

foot to the other. 'Bog off, Dad!'

'Don't do this, precious. Let me drive you up there, darlin'.'

Harley was standing – or rocking, to be more accurate, on the pavement at the bottom of the steps to Snaresbrook Tube station. She could not have looked more tormented if an army of ants had invaded her shoes and begun nibbling their way through the flesh of her feet.

'If you hadn't made that cow Rita buy these shoes, I wouldn't be like this, would I?' she railed. 'It's all your fault.'

'Angel, you said you wanted to wear sophisticated commuter clothes. Be reasonable, darlin'.'

Harley considered she was being very reasonable – in the circumstances. She didn't know why she couldn't wear trainers to work. Even the DMs that Miss Pincher grudgingly allowed her to wear for school would've been better than the ridiculous instruments of torture that Rita had forced her feet into. And as for the suits that she'd made her buy! She wriggled the waistband trying to find a bit of give but to no avail.

'These stupid clothes are unnatural, that's what they are!' she shouted. 'When I'm running the firm, I'm gonna make it compulsory to wear tracksuits to work.'

Harry leaned across the leather seats of the metallic blue Rolls Royce towards the open window and mopped his brow. 'Darlin', it don't work like that in our business. The punters won't respect you if you wear a tracksuit. Trust me – Rita knows what she's doing.'

'They'll respect me! Now clear off! You're making me look like some nerdy little wimp what needs 'er old man to drive 'er everywhere.'

Harry sighed, heavily. 'All right, my angel but remember what I told you, if you see the Bent gel, be nice to 'er. Let bygones be bygones, eh?' Harry looked as though an idea had just occurred to him. 'Tell you what, swede 'art, why don't you invite her round for a game of tennis one evening? How's that sound?'

'Oh, ha ha! Very flamin' funny!' Harley snarled. 'I'm walking like a ruddy crab with corns and you want me to invite that cow round so she can thrash me on my own ground? Nice one, Dad!'

'Darlin', darlin', darlin',' Harry cajoled. 'I just want you to be nice to her, all right? Talk to her. Find out what's happening with her and her brothers. Look on it as part of your work experience, eh?'

'I'm sick of this poxy work experience,' Harley sulked. 'It's boring. I want to go back to the tennis club.' A stab of pain shot across her foot between blisters, causing her to go over on her ankle and yelp with pain. She kicked off her shoes and threw one against the side of her father's car in anger and embarrassment.

'Darlin', darlin' – mind the motor, my angel.'

Mercedes rounded the corner and recognised the electric blue car instantly. It had disgraced the school car park on many a parents' evening and sports day. She hesitated; although sucking up to Harley Spinks had been phase two of Operation Stitch-up, doing so in front of her father was an entirely different game of tennis. She'd planned to seek out Harley, win her confidence over the next couple of mornings and then set up a meeting later in the week, so that she could infiltrate the firm's office. But, with Old Man Spinks on the scene, Mercedes wasn't so sure. Harley she could manage, but her father? She knew when she was playing out of her league.

Too late. Just as she had decided to hover out of sight until the coast was clear, Harley looked up and saw her. 'What're you staring at?'

Mercedes forced a smile which broadened into a genuine one as she mentally awarded Fern full marks for her assessment of her arch-rival's dress sense. Harley was dressed from head to foot in black and, just as Fern had reported, her two-piece looked more suited to issuing parking tickets than gracing any office. And, despite the fact that it was July, her muscly tennis-player's legs were shrouded in industrial strength tights. The only remotely elegant part of her attire was the footwear that she was currently waving in her father's face and even that wouldn't have looked out of place on Jenny's Mum. Seeing Harley in everyday clothes, Mercedes suddenly found herself experiencing an unprecedented wave of sympathy for the girl.

'Just concerned that you seem to have hurt yourself.'

'Yeah, right!' Harley sneered. 'Gloating, more like.'

Perhaps, Mercedes thought, she should reassess the whole sympathy thing. Ignoring the remark, she learned in front of her schoolmate and spoke through the open car window.

'Good morning, Mr Spinks. How are you today?' No point in pussyfooting around.

Harry was taken aback at her forward approach. 'Erm, I'm all right, darlin', and yourself?'

'Very well, thank you.' She turned to Harley, 'Fern said that you were working in the West End now, do you fancy travelling up together?'

Before Harley could reply, her father jumped at the suggestion. 'That would be nice, wouldn't it, my angel?' Harley glowered at him. 'Tell you what,' he continued, 'I was just going to give Harley a lift, weren't I, swede 'art? We could drop you off too if you wanted.'

Mercedes hovered for a second: there was something fishy about this. She weighed up the odds – the chances of Harry Spinks performing an act of kindness to anyone, let alone a member of the Bent family, were about the same as Chubby becoming president of MENSA. So, could it be a ploy to kidnap her and get back at her brothers? No chance! There was no way Harry would do his own dirty work and certainly not from such a public place. No, kidnapping was a rank outsider. But there was definitely something suspicious about the offer and the clever money had to be on Spinks having found out that she was working in the bank. So, she thought, he was hoping to pump her for information, was he? Well, two could play at that game.

'Excellent!' she opened the door and slid along the back seat while Harley took her place in the front. 'So, Harley, how's your work experience going? Mine's really boring, I just sit and watch this old biddy all day. How about you? What sort of things are you doing?'

As Harley grunted her response, Mercedes noticed

a scrap of paper on the floor of the car by her foot. Whilst pretending to listen, she made a show of putting down her bag then, surreptitiously picked up the note and slipped it inside; it could be absolutely nothing but you never know what might come in useful.

By the time the Rolls Royce turned off Pall Mall into St James's Square, Mercedes had managed to keep up an almost relentless stream of chatter without volunteering a single piece of information that Harry couldn't have found out by interviewing the bank's cleaner.

'Well, thank you very much, Mr Spinks,' she said, stepping out of the car. She was frustrated not to have made more headway with Harley. Had she been travelling on the Tube, as she'd planned, she would have suggested meeting up with her later in the week but she didn't want old man Spinks getting a whiff of what she was up to.

'Pleasure, darlin'. A pleasure. Tell you what, swede 'art,' he offered as she turned to walk away, 'why don't you come over to our place one night after work – 'ave a swim or a game of tennis or something? You an' my Harley ought to get to know each other a bit. You can . . . do whatever you gels do.'

'Dad!' Harley snarled. 'I told you to leave it out.'

Mercedes smiled. Did he think she was stupid? No way was she going to go waltzing into maison Spinks under the watchful gaze of Harry and his minders. No, far better for her to execute her plan via Harley alone.

'Thank you. Maybe next week, once we're back at school.' By that time, if everything went as she hoped, Harry would be safely behind bars and, as his piranha of a daughter seemed even less keen on the idea than Mercedes, the occasion would never arise. 'I'll tell you what though,' she said to Harley, 'why don't we meet up and go shopping or something after work?'

Harley glared at her. 'Yeah – 'cos trailing round shops is my favourite pastime.'

'I was thinking maybe we could find you some trendier business clothes. I know our work experience is nearly over but I expect you'll be helping your dad out quite a bit over the summer.'

'Diamond idea!' Harry beamed. 'Ain't it, swede 'art?'

Harley made a porcine sound that Mercedes took as being affirmative.

'Excellent!' she said. 'Thursday's late-night shopping, so let's go then. I might as well come to your office and pick you up. How's that sound?'

As the Roller purred away round St James's Square, a nervous quiver ran through her. The words *baby*, *candy* and *taking from* had never seemed more appropriate and yet, it had seemed too easy. Mercedes knew that the success or failure of her plan hinged on Thursday evening's shopping spree, or at least the few minutes she would have in Spinks's office before that; she just hoped Harry Spinks wasn't thinking along the same lines.

She waited on the steps of the bank watching the car glide out of sight before taking the piece of paper from her bag. It was a 'to do' list and, at first glance, appeared to be of little consequence:

take books to Manny

check tyres & oil

phone Jonnie

buy dog food

phone tennis Club re: Sergio

speak to Rita about H.

On closer inspection, though, Mercedes smiled with satisfaction. She must remember to take it with her when she went to see En Min this afternoon. In En Min's hands that little scrap of paper could prove to be very useful – very useful indeed.

Thirteen

Mercedes stood on the pavement and stared at the seedy looking doorway that was squashed between a sandwich bar and a bespoke tailor's shop on Wardour Street. The top part of the door was glazed with frosted glass and the lower panels were flaking brown paintwork. The words 'Spinks Org.', could just be discerned in peeling gold paint across the glass. She looked up and down the street in disbelief. Was that it? It looked more like the entrance to a second-rate dental practice or the call centre for Down and Out Minicabs Ltd than the headquarters of Harry Spinks's underworld empire.

She had, as planned, taken the architects' drawings to En Min's work placement on the Monday afternoon, together with the list she'd found in Harry Spinks' car. En Min had come up trumps with the copying of the plans and had produced a masterpiece in the transcription of Sid's shifts, rewriting them in the same handwriting as Harry's 'to do' list. Mercedes was satisfied that all the paperwork was now sorted; there were copies of the documents from

Frankie's office, reworded and rewritten to eliminate every possible reference to the Bent brothers or their firm, as well as a couple of others that made sure Spinks was implicated, not simply as an outsider who intended to cut in on someone else's job but as the mastermind behind it.

The originals had been safely returned to Frankie's office, but not without a few seconds of panic when Cheryl's Shogun had pulled into the drive just as Mercedes was closing the front door behind her. Fortunately, some quick thinking and the explanation that she'd come to look for an earring, supposedly lost whilst babysitting the previous evening, had allayed any suspicions her sister-in-law might have had.

So, everything was going according to plan. There was just this one last piece to put in place. She stood at the opposite side of the street from the Spinks Organisation office and took a deep breath. This was it; the last furlong. She carefully pulled a pair of cream cotton gloves from the rigid paper carrier she had with her. Every fingerprint had already been eliminated from all the plans, drawings, notes and schedules: no point in plastering them all over Spinks' office. She stretched her fingers into the gloves and grimaced; they might have been high

227

fashion when her nan was her age but they looked more like something Chubby wore to dust down the snooker table in the games room at home. No matter: the last thing she wanted was to incriminate herself at this stage of the game. She crossed the road and rang the intercom.

Once inside, she mounted the stairs slowly, taking care not to touch anything; not for fear of leaving fingerprints but because that morning she'd made the mistake of wearing a Karen Millen cream two-piece to work and there was every chance that it would end up looking like one of the towels she used to dry the dogs after they'd been romping in the muddy lake, if she allowed her sleeve to touch the walls. The plain emulsioned walls were the colour of old nicotine and dust balls drifted down the treads like tumbleweed. This was not what she'd expected at all.

'Hin 'ere, dear,' a woman called.

Tentatively, Mercedes pushed the Bakelite door handle and entered a large room that was lined with shelves, all heaving with an unruly assortment of books, ledgers and files. They seemed to be in no sort of order but were falling at angles as though they'd been tossed randomly and filed wherever they'd landed. An enormous desk in the centre of the room was barely visible beneath the reams of paper that cascaded on to the floor. Mercedes looked round in disbelief: *Spinks Organisation*? Disorganisation, more like!

On second thoughts though, this would do nicely. She recalled an old joke her father had once told her: Where do you hide a stolen elephant? Answer: on a game reserve! As a child, she hadn't understood but, standing in the midst of this wastepaper fest, it had suddenly become very clear – concealing the documents in this mess would be as easy as hiding a blade of dried grass in a haystack. All she needed was a few seconds on her own.

There was no sign of Harley but an older woman was standing behind the desk with her back to the window. Mercedes was struck by the incongruity of the woman's appearance. She had dyed orange hair and scarlet nails, yet she was wearing a navy blue trouser suit that would not have looked out of place on board a Royal Navy destroyer and she had a cigarette dripping from the corner of her mouth.

'Take ha seat, darlin'. 'Arley'll be wiv you hin a mo.'

Mercedes looked round for somewhere to oblige but there wasn't a seat to take that wasn't under at least four inches of papers. Perhaps, she thought, this was her chance? She lifted up the sheaf of letters, files and folders from one of the wooden chairs by the bookshelf and was about to lower herself on to the seat when she saw the dust on the back of the chair. So much for wearing a cream suit to work. Still, there was nothing else for it. She dropped her carrier to the floor, sat on the filthy seat and placed Harry Spinks's papers on her lap. She hoped her brothers would, one day, appreciate what she was doing for their sakes.

'She won't be ha sec,' the woman puffed at her through the smog of her cigarette, ' 'er dad wanted ha word before she left.'

Her dad! It hadn't occurred to Mercedes that Harry Spinks might also be there. A swarm of butterflies scrambled for take off in her stomach. She would not be sorry when all this was over.

The telephone rang and the woman behind the desk picked it up. 'Good hafternoon, Spinks Horganisation.'

Whilst she was speaking, Mercedes slipped the folder of evidence out of the carrier bag and pushed it into the middle of the pile on her lap. By the amount of dust on the chair those files probably hadn't been touched in months, so she was fairly sure no one would notice an extra one. So far, so good.

' 'Arry!' the woman bellowed in the direction of the landing. 'Hit's your waife!'

Mercedes had seen Harley's mother at school functions and had often felt sorry for the woman. Quite pretty, in a drab sort of way, she usually trailed her husband and daughter at a distance of a few feet, merging into the background like a shadow. Mercedes listened as the orange-haired woman spun the caller a well-practised pack of lies.

'Yays, she's getting hon fine, Fay . . . Yays, I'll be very sorry to see 'er leave tomorrow . . . Don't know what I'll do without 'er next week.'

Harry entered the room and forced a grin at Mercedes. 'Orright, darlin'?'

Mercedes smiled as disarmingly as she was able. 'Is Harley ready yet, Mr Spinks?'

'Nearly ready, swede 'art. She's a bit emotional what with tomorrow being 'er last day working wiv Rita and all.' Emotional? Mercedes wondered what emotion that would be. In her experience, Harley Spinks' emotional spectrum extended from anger to abject outrage with nothing else even featuring. Before she could ponder further, her question was answered. Harley appeared in the doorway and tossed a handful of twenty pound notes at her father.

'You can take your poxy money and stuff it! I ain't going!'

'Angel . . .' Harry began.

'And I ain't no angel, neither!'

Never a truer word spoken, Mercedes mused.

' 'Arry,' the orange haired woman cut in, 'Fay wants ha word.'

'What's *she* want?' Harley screamed. 'If she's bleedin' well checking up on me again . . .'

'Swede 'art, that's no way to speak about your mother.'

'She's always on my bleedin' case!' Harley took a swipe at the wastepaper basket.

Harry rubbed his hand across his forehead and sighed. 'Tell 'er I'll ring 'er back, Rita.'

Mercedes watched the drama playing out before her as Harry dropped on to his hands and knees and began picking up the money whilst his daughter kicked out at anything within a seventy-deniered leg's length. Rita turned her back on the scene and appeared to be whispering something diplomatic into the receiver when another phone rang from underneath the papers on the desk.

'Look, I think it would be better if I went,' Mercedes suggested, pleased to have an opportunity to escape. 'Maybe we could do this another time?'

' 'Ang on darlin', 'ang on,' Harry said, his tone beginning to show the strain. He scrabbled through the papers on the desk trying to locate the source of the ringing.

'No, just clear off! I never wanted to go shopping in the first place,' Harley spat. 'And if you think I want to end up looking like some jumped-up extra from *ER* with an off-white skirt and off-white jacket and stupid off-white surgical gloves, you can think again.'

OK, so the gloves were not Mercedes idea of trendy either, but they'd served their purpose and there was no way she was going to admit that to Harley.

'It's called *haute couture*,' she explained, hoping to blind her with foreign phrases. Then added, with feigned regret, 'Oh, I'm sorry, you dropped French, didn't you?' She ducked as a well aimed hole-punch whistled by her head and crashed against the shelves sending several folders tumbling to the floor. Mercedes took her cue to leave. She stood up and replaced the pile of papers and folders, including the file with the faked evidence in it, back on the chair. 'Mr Spinks, I can see that you were right when you said Harley was feeling emotional, so I really think it would be better if I left now.'

Harry picked up the phone. ' 'Old on, will you?'

he said to the caller, then covered the receiver with his hand. 'Orright darlin'; probably best.'

'Yeah! Good riddance!' Harley sneered, picking up a stapler. Then, when the words had fully registered she turned on her father. 'Emotional? What d'you flamin' mean, emotional?'

Mercedes gave the pile of papers one last glance, checking that the folder with the Boreham's Bank information was in place, and then turned towards the door just as the metal stapler hit the wood of the desk.

'Hey, Mercedes!' Harley called.

Mercedes hesitated, anxiously. This could be one of three things. Harley was either taking aim ready to impale her on a paper knife, or had spotted the file, or was going to issue some cutting remark to try and beat her on the bitching stakes. Casting a glance at the chair she could see that it was undisturbed and Harley's hands appeared to be free of missiles, so her money was on the latter.

'Yes?'

'That poncey suit you're wearing's got a dirty great smudge across the back of it. Shame!'

As she was about to reply, her attention was attracted by the scene behind Harley. Harry Spinks was on his knees amidst an ocean of stationery, whispering harshly into the phone. 'I told you not to call here again . . . I don't give a monkey's . . . This is between you and the Twerp Twins, mate . . .' And, call it intuition, but Mercedes was fairly sure that he was making reference to her own brothers. Which meant that, unless she was barking up the totally wrong tree, the person on the other end must be the grass that she'd heard Frankie talking about. She hovered, pretending to look in her bowling bag for something.

'Thanks for letting me know, Harley,' she said, not paying the slightest attention to her schoolmate. 'I'd better drop it into the cleaners' tomorrow.'

Harry continued in hushed tones. 'No chance, mate . . . You got a problem, sort it with Batman and the Boy Wonder.' And then he let out the *faux pas* that she'd been waiting for. 'I told you, you're the only one what can crack the code, you plonker!' And he slammed down the phone.

So, Sid was the double-crossing turncoat, was he? She didn't know what she was going to do with the information but one thing was for certain, it would be of some use to somebody at some time over the next thirty-six hours, she'd put money on it.

'Bye!' Mercedes called, eager to put as much space between herself and the Spinks family as possible.

But, no sooner had she reached the bottom of the stairs than Rita's voice echoed down the narrow hallway. ' 'Ere, you've forgot something.'

Mercedes heart stopped. No! It couldn't be! She couldn't have been rumbled already.

'I don't think so.' She looked up and held out her hands, innocently. She was aware that she'd stopped breathing. It was too awful to contemplate that the last week might all have been in vain.

'What's this then?' Rita held out something that, in the dingy light was difficult to make out but – Mercedes' heart sank – it looked suspiciously like the folder.

The disappointment was too much; she was just going to have to resign herself to finishing her education in a young offenders' unit. It was as though her feet had donned lead trainers as she slowly made her way back up the dismal staircase. But as she neared the top she could see the object that was being flapped in her direction was not, as she had feared, the folder with the information, but the carrier bag she had brought it in.

'Thanks!' she blurted before almost running down the stairs and out of the door. As she strode purposefully towards Oxford Street and the Tube, she took off her gloves and tossed them into a litterbin then dusted down her skirt, letting out a long sigh of relief. How her brothers had sustained a life of crime for so long was beyond her. If this was an adrenaline rush, they could forget it. She'd rather poke herself in the eye with one of Nick the Bubble's Kalashnikovs than go through that again. But still, she was on the home straight now.

Sid checked his watch. It was ten to twelve. He put the top back on his thermos flask and watched as Pete, his young colleague, unwrapped the foil from his packed supper and bit into the cheese and pickle sandwich that his wife had made.

'You not eating yours yet, Sid?' Pete asked, his eyes glued to the film that was showing on the miniature television on the desk. It was next to a row of larger CCTV screens but, while the screen Pete was watching had scenes of screeching cars and people running in terror, the security screens showed a variety of rooms and corridors all totally devoid of human activity.

Much as Sid would have loved to be tucking into the pork and apple sauce sandwiches that his wife, Betty, had made for him, he knew, of course, that there was little point. In just under ten minutes' time anything that went into his stomach now would be coming back up with the help of Tone's boot. He just hoped the lad wasn't too conscientious about his work.

'Saving mine till later, mate,' Sid replied, ignoring the echoing rumblings from his digestive system. Then preparing the way for what he was about to suggest, he said, 'Cor, my knee ain't half giving me some gyp tonight. That eleven o'clock round's done it in again. You wouldn't mind doing the honours with the midnight round, would you mate?'

'Course not,' the younger man agreed. 'But can it wait till this finishes?' He nodded at the television.

'What time's that then?' Sid felt himself begin to sweat.

'Ten past.'

Sid's heart was racing. Ten past was no good. Pete had to be well out of the way and at the top of the building long before that. He unscrewed the flask and poured himself another cup of tea; his mouth was beginning to go dry with fear. Sid was starting to regret getting involved with this whole business. He should've been satisfied with what he had. He and Betty hadn't been that badly off before. All right, so he was pretty mad about being made redundant after all those years but he was still employable; he'd landed this job, hadn't he? It wasn't ideal but it had been OK here for a while. But oh, no – he had to go shouting his mouth off down the Snitch and Snake in Plaistow, didn't he? Moaning to Gary, his old mate, about how the money was peanuts and how he was working in a bank and could read the combination of the safe, so he could get in there and nick a big wodge if he wanted.

Him and his bragging! Of course, the next thing he knew, Gary's boss and his brother had gone round there to have a little chat and make him an offer he couldn't refuse. All he'd been able to think about had been a long overdue trip out to Sydney to see their daughter Lorraine and her little girl. Their granddaughter was nearly seven years old and they hadn't even seen her yet – well, only on video.

But, what he hadn't known at that stage and what made matters a thousand times worse, was that the landlord of the Snitch was in arrears on his 'insurance' payments. So, instead of finding the cash from somewhere, he'd managed to get Harry Spinks off his back for a couple of weeks by offering him a little gem of overheard information in lieu of protection money. At first, Sid had thought that the whole thing looked pretty cushti – he was going to get two lots of money – one for doing the job and one for passing on the info. But now reality was starting to dawn. What if it went wrong? What if they got nicked? Getting a bit of a kicking is one thing, but getting banged up for a twelve stretch – well, that put a very different complexion on things.

He took a handkerchief from his pocket and wiped his brow. 'Sorry, mate. It can't wait really.'

'Aw – come on. Who's going to know if I'm a quarter of an hour late?' Pete stuffed the last crust of sandwich into his mouth.

Sid took another sip of tea and cleared his throat. 'There's cameras on us too, mate. The bosses'll know.' As long as he kept calm he'd be all right. He must keep a clear head.

'Tell you what, if you can manage this one, I'll do all the rest of the rounds – how's that?'

Sid checked his watch; it was five to. Pete should be setting off now and yet he was still glued to the television. Sid loosened his tie and ran his fingers round the inside of his collar. The basement suddenly seemed to have developed the atmosphere of a sauna.

'Can't do it, mate. My knee's been playing me up something rotten ever since I did the last one.'

Pete was becoming irritated. 'Bleedin' 'ell Sid – I've been watching this for an hour and a half. It's not much to ask.'

Sid was sure he heard a car engine running outside. Maybe he was imagining it. Pete hadn't responded, but then it was hardly an unusual event, to hear an engine running in the West End on a Friday night. He was getting paranoid. Although if Pete didn't get in that lift and disappear up to the seventh floor pretty soon, the reality would be a whacking great hole in the wall and both of them getting a good going over.

'What's the big deal? You know that his brother done it,' Sid said.

Pete sprang from behind the desk angrily. 'No, actually, Sid, I didn't know that his brother done it! Cheers!' He snatched the heavy blue jacket from the back of his chair and put it on. 'I don't believe you sometimes.' He pressed the button for the lift and the door opened immediately. 'If you've just done this so you can watch my telly . . . I'll . . . I will not be amused, Sid!'

The lift door shut removing Pete from the scene and propelling him to the seventh floor from where he would begin his descent, checking every room on every corridor for the next fifteen minutes. Almost simultaneously, Sid heard noises at the other side of the wall. Thuds sent a shudder through both Sid and the building then, within seconds, the bricks from which all but a few millimetres of mortar had been removed at the casino side, caved into the bank like a crumbling house of cards. They were off!

This was the moment Sid had been dreading; the moment he'd told Harry Spinks that he'd changed his mind about and had tried to negotiate a small fee and a ticket to Spain for the information he'd provided without having to be involved any further. But Harry wasn't buying it. 'And who the 'ell d'you think's going to crack the code, you plonker, if you've ridden off into the paella sunset?'

So, here he was and, even though he had been expecting it, the sight of two men in boiler suits and ski masks bursting into the basement of the bank caused Sid to put down roots and become paralysed to the spot at the security station. He stood, helpless with terror, as Tone ran to one side of the basement and sprayed paint on the security camera. Then, like a rabbit with myxomatosis caught in the headlights of an oncoming death-wagon, he stared, petrified, into the barrel of Frankie's AK47.

'Move it!' Frankie barked, waving the semi-automatic gun at Sid in a threatening manner – just for the benefit of the security cameras in the last few seconds before the paint dried.

But it was as though Sid was on intravenous Botox: not a muscle moved.

'I said – move it!' Frankie repeated.

Nothing. The other two men hovered, nervously. Sid remained behind the security desk, his eyes wide.

As soon as the cameras had been obliterated, Frankie took off his ski mask. 'It's me – remember? Now get over to the safe. We ain't got all day.'

Suddenly, Sid sprang into life and began flapping his arms in the air like an inept boy scout practising semaphore.

'For Gawd's sake! This ain't the flamin' Oscars.' Frankie thrust a pair of thin rubber gloves at Sid and almost dragged him across to the safe door. 'Get a grip,' he said, gruffly.

'Erm,' Sid puffed, placing his trembling fingers on the largest wheel of one of the combination locks, then stopped. Tone waited nervously as the older man hesitated. Frankie shot him a glare that would have cut through steel.

'You bottle on me now, Sid, and I'll make sure that a bottle's the only way you'll be taking your food for a long time – a very long time!'

'Seven to the left,' Sid spluttered.

Both men turned their combination wheels simultaneously.

'And, erm, three to the right.'

Again they moved in unison.

There was a crackle from Frankie's radio. He lifted it from the pocket of his overalls and pressed down the switch. 'What's wrong?'

Horace, who had parked round the corner after dropping off the others, spoke urgently. 'Old Bill!'

'What!' Frankie kicked the door of the safe in fury. 'Out! Out!' he bellowed.

'Hang on,' Horace's voice crackled. 'No, it's OK. They've gone past.'

Frankie flicked the switch. 'For Gawd's sake, 'Orace!'

'Better to be safe, Frankie.'

Frankie ran his hand across his brow then turned to Sid. 'Next!'

'Now, I think . . .'

'I told you before,' Frankie barked. 'I am the only one on my team what thinks – right? Now just give me the number.'

'Five left,' Sid blurted.

They turned the wheels and Frankie pulled the enormous steel door forward with ease. 'Nice one, Sid.' He turned to the others and indicated the pallets of bank notes before him. 'And now, gentlemen . . .' He grinned. '. . . Welcome to the pleasure dome. Let's get this lot shifted.'

Tone moved forward and spread an array of nylon bags on the floor of the vault. Hastily the three men pushed bundles of money into them. When the first two were filled, Tone picked them up and made towards the breach in the wall ready to transport them back up through the casino. The bags were going to be moved in stages; from the vault to the bottom of the casino stairs; up the stairs to inside the door and then, just as Horace pulled up, they would take them out into the street for loading into the getaway car.

'Move it!' Frankie yelled as Tone lumbered across the bricks and rubble that covered the floor.

But, as he reached the hole in the wall, there was a blinding flash of light.

Frankie left the vault and rushed forwards to investigate but reared back when a second flash filled the basement. 'What the—?'

Fourteen

The VW beetle was parked in the centre of St James's Square and, although Mercedes and Zak were posing as a courting couple, there was about as much passion happening in the car as there was on your average fishmonger's slab. Their attention was focused about fifty yards away on the building they'd both left only seven hours earlier. The square was eerily quiet compared to the bustle of the day and Mercedes was grateful that the dim street lighting afforded them some privacy. Her phone flashed up with a text message; it was Jenny.

Good Luck ☺

She smiled nervously and switched it off without replying.

Zak put his arms round her again to reassure her. 'It'll be OK.'

She bit her bottom lip; she wasn't sure. She hadn't heard anything to suggest that Harry Spinks had found the file, although she hadn't heard anything to say that he hadn't, either. But then, why would she?

As though reading her mind, Zak said, 'You don't think Harley Spinks could resist gloating if they'd found it, do you? Trust me, it's going to be all right.'

Mercedes nodded. Then another thought struck her. 'What if they've got a lookout posted by the door? I didn't hear Frankie saying anything about one in the plans but he might have thought of it later. No one in their right mind would do something like this without a lookout, would they?'

Zak moved away from her so that he could make eye contact. 'For starters, Frankie isn't in his right mind. And secondly, every criminal is caught out by two things: greed and arrogance. And your brother has both – in truck loads. He's too greedy to want to share his loot with an extra person and he's so arrogant that he probably thinks he's invincible. Don't worry.'

Mercedes nodded again.

As the clock on the dashboard clicked on to 23:59, a silver BMW drove into the square from the northerly direction and pulled up outside the casino. Mercedes leaned closer to Zak and pretended to be kissing him while she watched the proceedings over his shoulder. She felt as though someone had tied a reef knot in her stomach. This was it!

Two men emerged from the car dressed like workmen carrying tool bags. They looked so innocuous, they could have been emergency plumbers on a callout. The car drove off sedately round the square and the men nonchalantly approached the double doors of the casino. Suddenly, they dropped to their knees, pulled what must have been ski hats from their bags before donning them, then adeptly jemmied open the doors and disappeared inside without trace. They had taken only a few seconds and if, as Mercedes had overheard, the cameras on the bank were angled towards the main door and the ones on the casino weren't working, no one would even have been aware that they'd been there.

The alarm on Zak's watch bleeped just as the clock on the dashboard flipped on to 00:00. Mercedes straightened up.

'OK!' She tossed Zak a mobile phone, bought especially for the single call he was primed to make in one minute's time, then picked up her camera. 'If I'm not out in four minutes, go.'

'But—'

'Just do it.'

She got out of the car and shut the door without giving him a second look.

'Be careful!' he called but she was already halfway across the road.

The glass doors to the casino swung open easily and, once inside the building, she looked round for signs of a lookout. Zak had been right; what a fool Frankie was! She could have been the police, or one of Spinks' mob, or anyone. She knew the layout of the building from the architects' drawings and had no trouble making her way down to the basement, arriving at the hole through to the bank just as the unsuspecting Tone was heading back with the first bags of money. With a calmness that belied the squirming sensation in her stomach, she raised the camera to her eye and pressed.

Tone let out a gasp and Frankie ran forwards as she took a second photo.

'What the—?'

'Hi, Frankie.' She let the camera drop on to the strap round her neck.

Her brother lurched towards her in an attempt to grab the camera. 'Piss off out of here, Merce. You don't know what you're messing with.'

Mercedes stood her ground. 'Oh yes I do,' she said confidently. 'But I'm not sure I can say the same for you.' She looked at her watch. 'I'll be brief because, according to my calculations, in three minutes' time,

Uncle Horace will be arriving expecting to pick up you and the money, but he's going to be disappointed. The money isn't going anywhere near his car, it's going to be left on the pavement.'

Frankie's face contorted with anger. 'Get out of here, Merce – I'm warning you!'

'Or what, Frankie?' Mercedes challenged. Her heart was thumping so hard she was surprised it couldn't be heard at street level, but she knew it was imperative to stay cool. 'You see, at this very moment Cheryl is going through the contents of your study and destroying all the evidence that links you with this.'

'Cheryl?'

Mercedes put up a hand to stem his protest. 'But she might very well stop if I phone her and tell her about a certain supermodel you've been seeing.'

'You've got some front . . .'

Mercedes made a show of looking at her watch. 'Oh, look,' she said, 'time is ticking by. Best get on. So, I suggest you radio Uncle Horace and ask him to make it a little earlier because, as it stands, he's due to arrive at almost the same time as the Schizo Kid and . . .' She checked her watch again, pretending to count the minutes. '. . . the police.'

The two men behind Frankie looked at each other aghast.

'Why, you . . .' Frankie lunged forward again but Mercedes dodged him and he stumbled on a brick.

'They were phoned at one minute past midnight and I'm reliably informed by New Scotland Yard that an armed response unit will be here in about five minutes. I reckon the boys and girls in blue will also be going through Harry Spinks' office in Wardour Street at about the same time and guess what they'll find?' She didn't wait for an answer. 'Duplicates of all the documents that Cheryl is currently burning – with a few alterations, of course.' She looked round at the assembled faces of her brother's gang. 'Now, if you'll excuse me, I'm going to head off.'

She turned as she reached the bottom of the stairs of the casino. 'Oh, by the way, Kev isn't your grass; Sid is.' She looked through the gap and made eye contact with the security guard who was panting and gasping like an overfed turkey on the run up to Christmas. 'Sorry, Sid. I've made sure my family are OK but you're going to have to get yourself out of this one.' She nodded to Tone. 'I don't want any violence but I suggest you tie him up just to make it look authentic. Now, I'm pretty sure I can hear sirens so I suggest you scarper as soon as possible. Leave the money outside so that it looks as though Sabatini

251

and his gang did it and I'll meet you all at the lock-up at eleven o'clock tomorrow.'

Zak had moved the car ready to collect her and as soon as she was inside they drove around the square so that they could just see the bank.

'How'd it go?' Zak asked, pushing the gear stick into neutral but leaving the engine running.

'Ssh,' she said, turning round so that she could see the bank through the rear window. Seconds later the silver BMW screeched into the square and she saw two men appear from the casino and climb into the car before it sped away leaving several holdalls on the pavement. No sooner was it out of sight than a Lotus Elise squealed to a halt. Two men, both dressed in black leapt from the car and stood on the pavement scratching their heads. They peered at the bags and one of them kicked a couple as though suspecting some sort of booby trap.

'Open them, open them,' Mercedes willed under her breath.

She bit her lip. It was crucial that Jonnie Sabatini was found with the money in his possession, otherwise the whole operation could go pear-shaped. One of the men bent down, unzipped one of the bags and pulled out a bundle of money just as the square was filled with a cavalcade of flashing lights.

'Yes!' Mercedes punched the air. 'Result!'

Zak leaned over and kissed her. 'I know I've said it before, but I'm going to say it again; do we make a team, or do we make a team?'

'The Dynamic Duo has nothing on us,' Mercedes agreed. 'Now, let's get this Zak-mobile out of here – we've got an important meeting in the morning.'

At eleven o'clock, Mercedes squeezed Zak's hand and pushed open the door to the lock-up. Together they stepped over the metal threshold into the stark interior. If the temperature had been like a morgue the last time Mercedes had been there, it had now taken on the atmosphere of a Siberian morgue – in February – at midnight. At least part of the reason being the six pairs of hostile eyes that glared at them as they walked the length of the lock-up.

'Good morning,' she said, taking her place with the others around the trestle tables. Even Chubby looked at her angrily. Another squeeze of her hand from Zak gave her the confidence to continue. She tossed two photographs in to the centre of the tables. 'We got these developed at a twenty-four hour photo lab and the negatives are now in a safe place.'

Frankie picked up one, gave a snort of disdain and handed it to Horace.

Chubby took the other. 'It's a good one of you, Tone, but I don't think it does you no favours, Frankie,' he remarked.

Frankie snatched it out of his hands and threw it back on the table. 'What d'you want, Merce?'

At that moment the door to the lock-up opened again and the familiar shape of Laverne Bent was silhouetted in the doorway attempting to negotiate the six-inch high metal strip at the foot of the door. Her tight leather skirt restricted the leg movement in her knee area and her four-inch heeled mule sandals added the extra challenge of altitude.

'Bleedin' 'ell!' her voice echoed along the length of the vaulted workshop. 'Gizz an 'and then!'

Frankie looked from his mother to his sister and folded his arms defiantly but Chubby went to their mother's rescue. She was followed into the workshop by Molly who looked round and gave a nostalgic sigh.

'Blimey! It ain't changed a bit,' she said.

Laverne was less appreciative of their surroundings. 'What's going on? What is this place? And what the 'ell am I doin' 'ere on a Saturday morning when I could've been in bed?'

'It's my Gordon's old lock-up,' Molly replied, referring to her late husband. 'Him and Al started up 'ere.' She peered round the stark brick walls and oil-stained floor. 'I'd forgotten this place existed.'

'Forgotten?' Laverne queried. 'I never even knew. Another bleedin' secret your Al kept from me,' she said to her mother-in-law, accusingly.

'Mum. Nan,' Mercedes said, trying to call some sort of order to the assembly. 'There are going to be some changes around here and I want you all to know about them.'

'Oooo! 'Ark at 'er,' Laverne interrupted.

Ignoring her mother, Mercedes continued. 'It's come to my notice recently that my brothers have got themselves involved in activities that are against the law and that's going to stop.' Frankie groaned. 'As from now,' she said purposefully.

Slowly, Mercedes proceeded to go through the events of the past two weeks, mainly for the benefit of her mother and grandmother but also to let Frankie know the full extent of her knowledge.

'Good on ya, gel!' Molly applauded when Mercedes had finished. 'I wish I'd 'ad the bottle to stand up to my Gordon and your dad before they got in over their 'eads.'

'Thanks, Nan.' Mercedes looked to her mother. 'And I know you wanted Dad to retire because I overheard you and Auntie Sylvie talking at his funeral, so I can't believe you're happy about your sons following in his footsteps.'

Laverne, for once, seemed lost for words.

Mercedes addressed Frankie. 'While I was in your study investigating this robbery, I took the liberty of looking through your bank statements . . .'

'You nosy little . . . You had no right . . .'

'No, I didn't,' she agreed. 'But you had no right to try to steal the money that other people have worked hard to earn – so, in the greater scheme of things, I think my offence doesn't even come in the same league. Anyway, as I was saying; it's clear that in terms of what the bank knows about and the taxman is aware of, you are a substantially wealthy man. Yes?'

Frankie grunted.

'I don't know how you came by your money but the fact that what I saw was declared income suggests it's legitimate, so it's clear that you do not need to rob banks. So, from now on, you will not indulge in illegal activities. *Capisce*?'

Another grunt.

Molly Bent stepped forwards. 'You listen to me, Frankie – you should be thanking your sister, not grunting at 'er. You'd all be banged up, if it weren't for Merce.'

Frankie glowered at his grandmother but said nothing.

'And, while we're on the subject of sortin' stuff out, what's all this about you and this model woman? If you and Cheryl can't work out your differences, get a divorce. But you could do a lot worse than your Chel, so go and get yourself some relationship counselling or something first.'

Frankie threw his hands in the air in exasperation. 'Leave it out, Nan! Relationship counselling! Are you off your trolley?'

Molly leaned towards her grandson and wagged a threatening finger. 'Speak to me like that again, my boy and you'll be *on* a trolley – an 'ospital trolley.'

Frankie growled at her and took a cigarette out of his gold case.

Molly snatched it from his lips. She was on a roll. 'And you can pack that in an' all. If there's one thing worse for your 'ealth than crossing me, it's them things.' She tossed the cigarette to the floor. 'Now,' her voice softened as she turned her attention to her other grandson. 'Chubby: you got an 'eart of gold, son, but you give in to Frankie time and again – always 'ave done, ever since you was nippers.'

'You know what, Nan?' Mercedes suggested,

'I think Chubby would really benefit from some assertiveness training.'

'Assertiveness? Oh, I don't know about that, Merce,' Chubby said, diffidently. 'What d'you think, Frankie?'

Molly Bent raised her eyes in disbelief. 'Bleedin' 'ell, Chubby darlin', that's just what she's on about. You need to sort yourself out, son. That was a really nice gel you brought to my birthday, what do you think she'd say if she found out about your extracurricular activities?'

'Extra what?' Chubby asked.

Mercedes stifled an affectionate smile. 'It's OK, Nan, I can pick up some information about assertiveness classes from the community centre.'

'Cheers, darlin'.' Molly turned her attention to the oldest member of the gang. 'Now, 'Orace – what can I say? You've probably seen enough porridge to put you off Quaker Oats for life. And, I know Sylvie ain't my flesh an' blood but I'm fond of the gel and the reason she ain't here this morning is 'cos she's working her fingers to the bone in the salon – supportin' you and your criminal activities!' She shook her head, sadly. 'It ain't on, 'Orace.'

Horace's mouth opened and then closed again.

'Now, I know Sylvie's wanted a nipper for a long

while, only there's no one to run the salon if she 'ad to leave, so why don't you get yourself down the Technical College and enrol for a GNVQ in 'airdressin' – soon as possible.' Horace ran his hand over his bald head and opened his mouth to protest but Molly was unstoppable. 'So that just leaves the rest of you.' She looked from Tone, to Kev, to Gary. Sid was noticeable by his absence. 'If my grandsons ain't paying you a wage you can live on, tell 'em for Gawd's sake – or even withhold your labour . . .'

'Jeez!' Frankie interjected.

Molly raised an eyebrow to silence him. 'Don't forget, Frankie, Old Gaffer Spinks' lad might be goin' down for the Boreham's job but Merce 'ere's got the evidence that would alter that, so you'd better watch your Ps and Qs.'

Mercedes picked up the photographs from the table. 'Thanks, Nan.'

'Yeah, but what about Harry Spinks?' Chubby asked. 'Ain't 'e gonna point the finger?'

Mercedes shrugged. 'I'm sure he'll try but with his record I'll bet a pound to a penny he goes down.'

Zak interrupted. 'But is that fair? He didn't actually do it.'

'True,' Mercedes reflected. 'But the intention was there and he would've gone down two weeks ago if he hadn't nobbled all the witnesses, so in the long run I think he's got what's due to him.' She felt a sudden wave of relief that it was all over. 'Zak and I have a function to attend with Zak's family – but just before we go, there's one more thing, Frankie.' Her brother groaned again. 'There's a girl in my class, Fern Simmonds. Her parents died a few years ago and her aunt can't afford her school fees. I've been running a sweepstake to subsidise her but I think it would be nice if you started to give something back to the community. Take care of it till she leaves, will you?'

'Course 'e will, babes,' Molly said, kissing her granddaughter on the cheek. 'Now, be off with you and 'ave a nice time. You done good, Merce.'

Zak grinned. 'Nice meeting you all,' he said and they made their way out of the lock-up.

' 'Ere, where you off to? You can't just call a meet then swan off like that,' Laverne called after them. 'You come back 'ere.'

'Leave the gel alone,' Molly cut in. 'She done what you and me should've done years ago. You raised a good 'un there, 'Verne.'

Laverne cocked her head on one side, thinking about her mother-in-law's words and then decided to agree with her. 'Yeah, I 'ave, ain't I? She done us proud – bless!'

Once in the car Zak put his arm round Mercedes' shoulder and kissed her. 'I am so proud of you.'

Mercedes smiled. 'Thanks – I couldn't have done it without you.'

'What do you think'll happen to Harley Spinks if her dad goes down?' Zak asked, slipping the car into gear.

Mercedes shrugged. 'I haven't a clue, but her mum's not so bad. Maybe they'll have the chance to get to know each other a bit better with Harry out of the way.'

Zak smiled. 'Could be your chance to win the tennis cup, if she's out of sorts.'

Mercedes shook her head. 'No way! Harley'd still be favourite if she had three left feet and one arm tied behind her back. But either way, when I do beat her, I want it to be fair and square.' She squeezed Zak's hand and returned his smile. 'Anyway, I don't want to talk about Harley Spinks – tell me about this party we're going to.'

The car pulled away from the lock-up. 'It's another of my cousins. He's a futures broker in the city.'

Mercedes thought for a moment. 'A futures broker? What's that?'

'He invests other people's money in things that he thinks might happen in the future – stuff like whether or not it's going to be sunny in Guatemala next month or how much oil a certain country might produce.'

Mercedes nodded. 'And he does that for a job?'

'Yes.'

'With other people's money?'

Zak eyed her questioningly. 'What's going on in that head of yours?'

Mercedes grinned. 'I'm just thinking that it sounds like my kind of job. I'm wondering why the old bird didn't fix me up with a futures broker for work experience.'

'Good job she didn't,' Zak chuckled. 'I might never have met you. But, if you want to talk futures, what odds are you offering on ours?'

Mercedes leaned back and gave him a satisfied smile. 'Oh, I think it's definitely worth a flutter.'

A note from the author

When I first began writing *BLAGGERS* I wasn't sure how I was going to do it, because foiling a bank robbery wasn't something that had ever featured on my `things-to-do-before-I-die' list. I knew absolutely zilch about criminals and crime fighting. But doing the research has been one of the most interesting and enjoyable parts of creating Mercedes' story. In fact, I probably now know more than is healthy for an ordinary, law-abiding citizen!